The Stalker Chronicles

D0888052

The Stalker Chronicles

Electa Rome Parks

www.urbanbooks.net

Urban Books, LLC
78 East Industry Court
Deer Park, NY 11729

The Stalker Chronicles Copyright © 2012 Electa Rome
Parks

All rights reserved. No part of this book may be re-
produced in any form or by any means without prior
consent of the Publisher, except brief quotes used in
reviews.

ISBN 13: 978-1-60162-334-8
ISBN 10: 1-60162-334-8

First Trade Paperback Printing February 2012
Printed in the United States of America

10 9 8 7 6 5 4 3 2 1

Distributed by Kensington Publishing Corp.
Submit Wholesale Orders to:
Kensington Publishing Corp.
C/O Penguin Group (USA) Inc.
Attention: Order Processing
405 Murray Hill Parkway
East Rutherford, NJ 07073-2316
Phone: 1-800-526-0275
Fax: 1-800-227-9604

The Stalker Chronicles

Electa Rome Parks

Dedication

This is dedicated to each of you who realize the power and beauty of having a dream. I'm a witness to the fact that they do indeed come true. Dream on . . . and above all, make it happen.

Epigraph

I hope you can't sleep and you dream about it. And when you dream, I hope you can't sleep and you scream about it. I hope your conscience eats at you and you can't breathe without me.

—Eminem, "Stan"

Acknowledgments

*God can dream a bigger dream for me, for you,
than you can ever dream for yourself.*
                                    – Oprah

Hello, family!

How you doin'? (*Asked in my best Wendy Williams voice.*) Who would have thought that the shy, skinny little girl from Georgia would, as an adult, release book number eight—the one you're holding in your hands?

Believe me when I say that all I've ever wanted to do was to write entertaining stories that captivate readers and introduce them to all the imperfect characters who live in my head. That's all I've ever wanted: to have a voice. A voice that is strong, solid, and true. It means the world to me to be allowed to enter your homes, and hopefully your hearts, as I give life to my unforgettable characters, who become like family to me during the course of penning the story.

Well, my girl Pilar is back! Yeah! You, my fabulous readers, asked for another storyline centered around her, and I listened. I have to admit that Pilar has become one of my favorite characters to date. There's something exhilarating about living vicariously through the antics of a "bad girl" (this coming from the classic Goody Two-shoes, myself). Pilar is the woman you guys love to hate, but secretly root for. However, for me, Pilar is simply misunderstood (LOL).

Acknowledgments

With that said, grab your favorite snack, pour a generous glass of wine and keep the bottle within arm's reach, and get ready for a wild roller-coaster ride that you won't soon forget. Pilar is back, and she demands attention. Now, get to reading.

Before you go, I guess I had better get to thanking a few people. As always, thank you, my dear readers, for supporting and encouraging me, for reading, and for being a source of joy in my life. It has truly been a highlight of my life to meet you at book signings, literary conferences, and libraries, and on Facebook. To the book club presidents and members, you guys know I simply adore you as my literary ambassadors, who put the word out, good or bad. I've enjoyed meeting you, coming into your homes and venues over the years, and bonding through our love of reading, words, and books. Oh, and what happens at the book club meetings stays at the book club meetings☺.

To my wonderful family and close friends, I love you guys, and thank you from the bottom of my heart for being my strength, my joy, my anchors, my dream encouragers, and my sounding board for this crazy journey that I've brought you along for the ride. Nelson, Brandon, Briana, Tresseler, DeJuan, Jordan, Khai, Laymon, Buffie, Pam, Audrey, Sharron, Leida, and Sandra . . . thank you, thank you, thank you. Muah. Hugs and kisses.

To Portia Cannon (agent) and the Urban Books family (Carl, Natalie, and Diane), thank you for giving my "talent" a home and a platform on which to be heard.

Special thanks to my author friends and industry buddies for always being in my corner, supporting me, encouraging me, and listening to my venting (and, boy, can I vent): Cheryl, Cydney, Eric, Vincent, Marissa, GA Peach authors, and Ella. To anyone I may have missed, please charge it to my mind and not my heart.

Acknowledgments

Readers, drop me a line at novelideal@aol.com and sign my guest book at www.electaromeparks.com. By now you know that I love to hear from you and read your feedback and comments. And, yeah, I'm still sensitive about my stuff☺. Don't forget to post your reviews on Amazon.com and BarnesandNoble.com; they really do make a difference. Be sure to check out and enjoy my previous titles as well: *The Ties That Bind, Loose Ends, Almost Doesn't Count, Ladies' Night Out, Diary of a Stalker, True Confessions,* and *These Are My Confessions* (anthology). And last but not least, please do *not* share your books. Encourage potential readers to purchase their own copies so that you can continue to read stories by your favorite authors by increasing our sales. In this business, it is all about the sales.

Also, visit me at:
www.facebook.com/electaromeparks and
www.electaromeparks.blogspot.com.

Until next time, I pray your life is filled with peace, love, and joy. Remember, there is only one thing greater than yourself. . . .

Stay blessed, always.

Electa
Signing off, Atlanta, August 19, 2011, 2:14 A.M.

Prologue

It was getting easier and easier now.

She moved quickly and efficiently throughout the spacious three-car garage. She wanted to remove any traces of evidence that she had ever been there. She had always been good at simply disappearing and being invisible. That was easy.

She was definitely more confident, and it showed in her cool, calm, and collected demeanor. She was no longer afraid of being caught, because the urge to punish those who had hurt her was stronger, much more overwhelming, and urgent. She probably couldn't stop herself even if she wanted to—she was operating on pure animal instinct. The need to survive and protect herself by any means necessary overrode anything else. Fight or flight. And she had long been tired of running.

There had been others over the years, more than she could count on one hand. They were mere vague gray memories that occasionally crossed her mind, like one might think of a stray pet one owned as a child, but she dismissed the images just as quickly. She never held on to them for more than a few fleeting moments in time. Denial was her refuge.

Only one had successfully escaped her sharp talons and womanly wiles. Or had he? Maybe she let him get away, just that one time. She hadn't determined which. Sometimes she thought of him, when her mind wasn't a jumble of darkness, discontent, and madness. There were moments. . . .

She missed him, yearned for his special touch, the touch that only he could deliver with precision and skill. His touch brought heat and desire. His lies brought pain and sorrow. She hated that he escaped her grasp, or that possibly she let him walk away, unscathed. She still considered him her soul mate, the one who made her complete and safe and sound. She yearned to feel complete, because most days she realized she was broken and damaged beyond repair. However, she couldn't think of that one just yet. Not now. That would come later. The strenuous act of positioning this one just right was over. Now she had serious, delicate cleanup work to complete. Within seconds, that one, the one who got away, was pushed to the dark, cold recesses of her mind. Forgotten . . . for now.

It was painstakingly slow work because everything had to be absolutely perfect. She had observed and respected what a perfectionist he was. He thrived on it. She softly snickered to herself and had to catch herself before it became an all-out rambunctious laugh. He didn't look too perfect right now, slumped behind the steering wheel of his black BMW like a deflated, tossed-aside bag of rags and bones. Another snicker escaped. She tightly clamped her gloved hand down over her mouth to stop it, to keep it from spilling forth.

When he was discovered—hopefully, within a day or two—she wanted him to appear perfect in death. That was the least she could do, because she honestly felt she owed him that much. With a gloved hand, she carefully took the typewritten note out of his jacket pocket, typed from the personal computer in his home office, and gently placed it next to him on the soft leather passenger seat of his car. Laughter escaped freely and drifted into the still air.

She took one last hopeful look at him and placed a single kiss on his left cheek. She wanted to remember him at peace. Happy. So handsome. She sighed before she carefully closed the driver's side car door. Then she continued to wipe down any surface she might have touched that bore her prints. She was patient as perspiration dotted her forehead. From her experiences, she knew that patience was a virtue.

She dreamily thought, We could have been so deliriously happy together. They always fucked things up. Always. She hadn't met a man yet who didn't. It was never a matter of if, but when. If only he hadn't started to question or doubt her because of that damn movie, *Diary of a Stalker,* which had been released a month earlier and was a blockbuster success. Everyone was talking about it; already there was talk of Oscar nominations for best actress and best actor. She couldn't escape it, no matter where she turned or what it signified for her.

No, you didn't reject me and attempt to walk away, without a backward glance, she thought. How dare he? She didn't do well with rejection. Never had. Never would. She chuckled to herself, thinking the joke was definitely on him. If he were alive, he would probably appreciate the joke as well. She had decided years ago that no one, especially not a man, would ever hurt her again. Never again. So far, she hadn't broken her promise to herself, nor did she have any intentions to going forward.

She exited the beautiful, spacious home that screamed quiet elegance, luxury, and money. She let herself out and quietly disappeared into the night, under the cover of darkness. She craved the darkness for its mystery and power. She whistled a happy tune to herself as she walked away. No worries. No rush. She was lost in her own demented world. *Enter at your own risk.*

She reminisced about a man—a beautiful, tall, dark, and very sexy man with deep dimples and gorgeous teeth, a man she couldn't wait to be reunited with. Her body craved him, and she could hardly contain her excitement and joy at just the mere thought of being in his presence again. It had been too long. As for the one in the garage, with the car engine running and the towel stuffed in the exhaust system, he had already slipped her mind, before his body was even cold and stiff. Her last thoughts of him were that when they found him, she hoped he would look perfect. She knew he would want it that way. After all, that was the least she could do. She hummed a lively tune and strolled off into the darkness.

Chapter 1

Xavier

In retrospect, what could I say? The last couple of years had not been the best moments of my life, definitely nothing to brag or write home about. They had been more like bittersweet years, an odd combination of sweet and sour moments.

Life could send some toxic shit your way that had you hanging on for dear life by a thin thread, hoping and praying that you'd come out on the right end. I sometimes felt like I had almost drowned and needed to be resuscitated, but the fear of going under water, of being helpless, remained with me. I had gone from having it all, at least by my standards, to being reduced to my lowest in only a matter of months.

Pilar was my personal joy stealer. My scab. Yes, let's place a name on it. She definitely received her wish. She was always on my mind, the last person I thought about each night before I closed my eyes and the first person I thought of as I rose each morning. I had gone over it again and again in my mind, breaking it down to its most organic level, but I could honestly say I never saw her coming in a million years, or at least what she had in store for me. Lust and desire blinded me, and that became my eventual downfall.

You see, Pilar was the beautiful, stunningly sexy, and confident woman who stalked me for nearly a year after we had a one-night stand, multiple times. I was in lust, and she was in love. However, I soon learned that rejection and craziness to the ninth degree were a lethal combination. She almost succeeded in making me lose everything dear to me, even my dignity and pride. Pilar brought me to my knees, literally, and made me rethink male/female relationships in general. I now knew to never, ever judge a book by its cover. That was pretty ironic since I was a national bestselling author with seven published novels, one of which had recently been made into a blockbuster movie. However, it was true, looks could be deceiving. *All that glitters is not gold, unless maybe it's fool's gold.* I was definitely the fool. I played right into Pilar's demented hands.

I was trying desperately to get my life back on track but was finding that was easier said than done. *Diary of a Stalker,* the movie, was released a month ago, and the reviews and box office sales were amazing. People all across the nation were embracing my true-to-life account that chronicled how Pilar stalked me and made my life a living hell. Reviewers were raving about how it was the modern-day version *of Fatal Attraction,* a late 1980s film starring Michael Douglas and Glenn Close.

I didn't know about all that, but looking back, I knew I was living in my own private hell, courtesy of Pilar. She was what true nightmares were made of. Not that fake shit we watched in a darkened movie theater for two hours as we snacked on buttery, salted popcorn and watered-down soda. No, Pilar was the real deal. I still woke up in cold sweats, frantically looking around my bedroom for looming shadows, things that go bump in the night, and straining to hear any unknown, unfamiliar sounds. Soon my erratic heartbeat would calm down, and eventually I would fall back to sleep after double-checking the locks on my doors and windows. Even though I had the best security that money could buy, I still checked . . . just to make sure.

I was forever mindful that Pilar was still out there, still insane, lurking in the shadows, and that terrified me like nothing else.

Chapter 2

Pilar

What a beautiful day, I thought as the first rays of sunlight drifted through the partially open mini blinds of my bedroom. I arose bright and early in a wonderful, cheerful mood and ate a hearty breakfast, which was something I rarely did. However, I was starving. I feasted on pancakes dripping in heavy syrup, eggs, and crispy bacon. Later I enjoyed a long, very hot shower. I dressed casually, then headed to my office at one of the top newspapers in L.A. This was something I rarely did, as well, worked from the office. I'd been hired a year ago, when I relocated from Houston to Los Angeles by way of a beautiful tropical island that shielded me from the unwanted media scrutiny.

Michael, my boss, the editor in chief, pretty much assigned me human-interest stories, and I went out, researched, completed the interviews, and e-mailed them into the office. They were mostly fluff stories. It worked for me and allowed me the luxury to work from home. I rented a two-bedroom apartment in downtown Los Angeles, not too far from my place of employment. Initially, I was hired to work in the office as one of the editors, but I soon realized it wasn't for me. I wasn't good at dealing with too many people on a day-to-day basis. I never had been. After Michael and I became intimate, he reassigned me. He was always trying to please me. He knew if I was happy, then he was very happy.

About an hour later, as I casually strolled into the office, I instantly knew something was wrong. The atmosphere was dismal. Many of the reporters and writers were clustered in groups, whispering quietly to one another. The always loud and vibrant office was gloomy and disjointed, with sad faces all around.

"Good morning," I said to everyone I passed before reaching the temporary cubicle in the corner, the one I used when I came into the office at least once a week.

"Morning," I heard a few reply halfheartedly. I turned to look in their direction with a scowled brow.

"Wow, it feels like a funeral up in here. What's going on?" I questioned, placing my leather purse down and walking over to the nearest group.

"Oh, my God, you haven't heard, have you?" Debra asked, looking at me in shock, utter disbelief, and amazement as she covered her dainty mouth with her right hand.

"Heard what?" I asked nonchalantly.

The circle of four became suddenly quiet.

"You haven't been watching the news?" the chunky, red-faced sports reporter asked.

"No. Over the weekends, I rarely even turn on my TV."

They curiously looked from one to the other, then back at me. The sports reporter, I think his name was Frank, dropped his head down and stared at the floor. He seriously looked like he was about to break into tears any minute.

Finally, the receptionist spoke up. "Pilar, I'm sorry to deliver the news."

"What news?" I asked, as if I had no clue as to what was going on.

She sighed and simply spit it out. "Michael is dead."

"What?" I cried out, trying not to be overly dramatic, but to have just the right amount of concern etched in my voice.

"He was found early Sunday morning," she volunteered.

"What? H—how? What h—happened?" I stuttered. In my mind I was thinking how I was putting on an Oscar-worthy performance. Look out, Halle Berry. Maybe I should consider acting in the land of wannabe actors and actresses.

"It was an apparent suicide. His mother found him in his car, dead from carbon monoxide poisoning. He had stuffed a cloth in the tailpipe so toxic fumes could enter his car and, of course, his lungs."

"He even left a note."

I didn't respond, simply willed crocodile tears to form. As I stumbled, the assistant editor caught my arm. I leaned on him for support and comfort.

"Are you okay?" he asked, pulling out the nearest chair so I could sit and catch my breath. My heartbeat was pounding away at a mile a minute.

"Yeah, I guess. This is such a shock."

"Tell us about it. We were all just saying that, how it is unbelievable," he added.

"I spoke with Michael on Friday regarding some edits for an article I was putting the finishing touches on. Wow, you never really know people," I said and shook my head slowly from side to side. "Unbelievable. And his mother found him?"

The female entertainment reporter didn't comment, simply looked at me oddly. *Simple bitch,* I thought. I knew Michael was fucking her, had been for a few weeks. I hoped she enjoyed my sloppy seconds, because I was definitely number one.

"This is so unlike Michael. He wasn't depressed. He wasn't withdrawn. He didn't have any of the classic symptoms of depression. I became close to him over the years, and he simply wasn't the type," the sports reporter revealed.

"The type?" I asked.

"The type to commit suicide. It just doesn't add up. In fact, he was scheduled to drop by my house on Sunday to watch the game and drink a few beers. Who makes plans when they have no intentions to be around in the next forty-eight hours?"

I nodded in agreement.

"You never know what's really going on in people's lives," the sports reporter said.

"You never know," I gushed.

"So true," the entertainment reporter stated, looking me up and down, from the top of my head to the tips of my toes, with her nose scrunched up, making it obvious she didn't like what she saw. She hadn't liked me from day one, and the feeling was mutual.

I glared back at her, met her eyes, and made her look down first. She couldn't step to me, and she knew it. If she didn't know, then she had better learn. I thought, *She won't be getting that dick anymore. Me, either, for that matter.* Michael was good, but I had had much better. A certain bestselling author came to mind, and I couldn't help but smile, but I bit the inside of my lip to turn the smile into a smirk.

All that occurred in the early morning, before lunchtime. Before the day was over, I resigned from my position and boarded a plane for Houston. Everyone would think I was distraught over Michael's apparent suicide. If only they knew. Los Angeles was okay, but I longed for Houston, or at least for a particular resident of that city. I couldn't wait, couldn't wait until he got ahold of me. The time was right for a reunion of sorts.

Chapter 3

Dre'

"Hey, man. I'll be at the spot in fifteen," I said to my lifelong best friend.

"That's what I'm calling about," Xavier said hesitantly.

"Damn, here we go again. I know you aren't canceling on me again," I stated, with clear frustration in my tone. This would be the third time in two weeks.

"Dre', man, I'm not going to be able to hang out tonight. Give me a rain check."

"You are starting to sound like a recording. The same old bullshit every time we are supposed to hook up."

"I—I'm not into—"

"Save it, save it, Xavier. I'm not asking much. I simply want my drinking buddy to swing by the bar, drink a few brews, and shoot the breeze. That's all. Nothing more, nothing less."

"I know, man, but I'm not up to that tonight, not feeling it. I think I'm going to chill out at home and have an early night."

"Aren't you going stir-crazy up in that joint? You act like a damn recluse. . . . All you do is write and chill out at home. I can't believe you came out of your cave for the *Diary of a Stalker* premiere."

"You're right."

"Damn, quit saying I'm right. There used to be a day when you would never admit to me being right. And listen to me. Got me sounding like I'm your bitch or something," I laughed.

We chuckled, and for a few minutes it was like the good old days, before a crazed stalker bitch lurked behind every bush, strapped with leather whips and a healthy dose of revenge heavy on her heart. There was a thin line between love and hate.

"I promise I'll swing by tomorrow, and we can shoot some hoops or play spades and throw something on the grill. There's nothing that beats hot food and cold brews," Xavier stated.

"I'm holding you to that, my brotha. You haven't had your ass beaten in some time, and I don't want you to forget what it feels like."

"You don't know what it feels like, either, because I've never had my ass beaten by you, my brotha," Xavier said and laughed.

"Yeah, whatever. You know the deal. Don't front. Who is the best basketball player between us? We've had this debate going ever since we were nappy-headed boys growing up in those rat-infested projects we called home."

"And I've been telling you since the first day I whipped your sorry ass all over the courts in the Bedford projects that I was."

We both laughed at the trash talk we liked to dish out on one another.

"Seriously, man. Check me out tomorrow. I realize you are settling back into living in Houston again after your extended stay in Los Angeles, where you guys were filming, but I miss you, man."

"And I miss you more, man," he joked back.

"I'll holla at you tomorrow. Beer is on you."

"Deal. Later."

"Hey, hey, Xavier," I screamed before he disconnected.

"Huh?"

"You know what you need, man?"

"What? Because I'm sure you're going to tell me even if I don't want to know."

"Get you a piece of ass, and I promise you, you'll feel ten times better by tomorrow."

"Man, you're a fool." He chuckled. "That was what got me in the mess I was in to begin with."

"That was some crazy-ass pussy. Get some that's sane."

"You ain't never lied."

"Ain't nothing like some new ass. It cures all. Some pussy a day keeps the doctor away."

"Later, man. You have lost your damn mind. Oh, I forgot. You ain't never had one."

I disconnected my cell phone, still chuckling to myself. We always seemed to act like teenagers when we were around each other.

Xavier and I went back many years; we grew up on the mean streets of Houston together. I was closer to that man than to some of my own relatives. We had been through a lot together, good, bad, and ugly. But through it all, our friendship and bond remained intact. I knew without a shadow of a doubt that I could count on him to have my back and vice versa. We just rolled like that.

My man had been through a lot the last couple of years—mainly because his dick made some bad decisions concerning this chick named Pilar. I sensed she was bad news from the start. I tried to warn my man, but his other head had a mind of its own. She turned out to be the stalker from hell, and she succeeded in turning his world upside down. Don't get me wrong; I had been through two bad marriages and two bad divorces, so I knew the power of the pussy. It could make the male species make some fucked-up choices, even when our brain was telling us to run like hell. Run like your life depended on it. In Xavier's case, it really did.

Anyhow, that was all water under the bridge now, because psycho had moved on, and my man was blowing up the big screen with a movie based on his true-to-life book, *Diary of a Stalker*. There was talk about some of the actors receiving Oscar nominations, and Xavier was paid. He had finally reached the level he had always talked about when we were growing up. All my man wanted to do was tell tall tales and make movies.

I couldn't be prouder of my friend, because he deserved this and had worked his ass off for everything he'd accomplished. I just wished I had the old Xavier back, the one before psycho Pilar blew in and caused havoc.

Chapter 4

Xavier

"Ohhh, baby, that's it. Suck it!"

"Like this?" she asked, just before squeezing down harder with her full, pretty lip-glossed lips.

"Damn, that's right! Just like that!"

"You like that, Daddy?" she cooed.

"I love it, baby! Goddamn!"

I leaned back in the chair I was sprawled in at the moment, completely nude, with my legs apart. She was buck naked, had a beautiful, curvaceous body, and was planted solidly between my legs, sucking my dick like it was nobody's business.

I reached forward to fondle her breasts and reveled in watching her in action. She was the best I had ever had when it came to oral skills, and I could not wait to reciprocate.

I grabbed the back of her head to force her to take in even more of my tool. She resisted for a fraction of a second and then opened her mouth wider. It was obvious she enjoyed giving head, and I could not be happier. It was heaven on earth.

"That's my girl. Lick my balls. Oh, hell yeah!"

Right before I closed my eyes, lost in another dimension, she pulled one hand away from my dick and inserted her own finger inside her womanhood. I watched in fascination as she continued to give me *head and played inside her pussy with one, then two slim fingers. A man could take only so much; I closed my eyes and let out a rip-roaring moan that surprised even me with its intensity as I released my warm liquid into her hot mouth. She eagerly swallowed and licked at the last drops that remained. I closed my eyes and savored the moment. I couldn't wait to get up inside her warm sugar walls and show her who the man was without uttering a single word.*

To my surprise, when I opened my eyes, she was still between my legs, but my bloody severed dick was in her hands.

"See I told you, Xavier, if I couldn't have it, no one would. This belongs to me and always will. Don't you ever forget it, either."

She proceeded to carefully place it in a ziplock baggie, then inside a black bag that I hadn't seen before. The black bag, with its precious cargo, was now mysteriously by her side and zipped up.

"You won't need it anymore, babe."

I couldn't speak; I could only look on in horror and disbelief. A silent scream was lodged in the back of my throat, unable to escape.

"I left your balls," she said. "If you don't want them, I can pack them up, too."

Just as I attempted to say something, anything, she kissed me on the lips, leaving a thick trail of blood, which dripped down my chin. Then she winked at me, threw her head back, and let out this crazy-ass laugh that sent chills up and down my spine.

Around that time, I woke up screaming like a bitch, tossing, and kicking at my sheets. It took me a few seconds to realize it was all a nightmare. However, that still didn't take away the effect it had had on me. With unsteady hands, I reached into my nightstand drawer, pulled out my bottle of liquor, and took a couple of quick swigs. I closed my eyes and relished the burn as the liquor went down. My breathing gradually returned to normal, and my heart slowed, after nearly jumping out of my chest. Slowly, my night terror passed.

After that, I knew I wouldn't be able to sleep anytime soon. I slipped on my boxers and walked downstairs to my home office—to write the night away. I would slip quietly back into bed as dawn approached, with dark circles under my eyes.

Dre' was correct in his assessment. I needed to reclaim my life before Pilar drove me crazy. What a damn shame that even with her out of my life, she was still creating chaos.

The Beginning

The adorable, chubby-cheeked young child knew from experience to remain quiet and still in her presence. Children were to be seen and not heard. She shyly peeked out of the corner of her eye at her—her mother.

They were sitting in the tiny living room, watching a sitcom on the small TV set. This was definitely a rare occasion, because her mother usually avoided her as much as possible when they were alone. Her mother, as usual, wore a scowl, a cigarette dangling precariously from her lips, and her right foot was in constant motion as she swung it back and forth in a nervous posture.

Anyone peeking through the open curtains would have thought this was a typical family evening, a beautiful young mother and a precious daughter enjoying a peaceful time together. However, the young child knew better. That lesson had been instilled in her early on, and she'd learned it well.

The evenings were always the worst. She always attempted to make herself invisible. She would pull her body into a small, tight ball of arms and thin legs. Poof! Gone. That was what she hoped for most nights: to simply disappear, to evaporate into thin air. She knew she wouldn't be missed. And that realization constantly shattered her heart into a million aching pieces. She longed to feel love and be loved. That was all she dreamed of.

Even in her immature mind, she knew mothers were supposed to love their children, nurture them, and protect them from evil. In this case, her mother was the evil.

Chapter 5

Pilar

Strange. It was like my soul sensed we were close to landing in Houston, Texas. I wondered if he sensed my presence. I wondered if the hairs on the back of his neck and on his arms stood up and came alive, as mine did, simply because we were breathing the same air again. I closed my eyes and moaned. I could feel him on my skin. Taste him in my mouth. Seconds before the pilot's voice came over the plane's intercom system, I awoke from a deep sleep, feeling totally refreshed and renewed.

I placed my seat in an upright position and then stretched as much as possible in my first-class seat and in the empty one beside me. That nap was exactly what I needed in order to rejuvenate myself. The fun was about to begin, and I needed all my strength to participate. Pulling out a small gold and black compact to freshen my makeup, I smiled to myself. It still shocked me when I looked into a mirror nowadays. For a few seconds I didn't recognize the person staring back.

A couple of years ago, when the entire media circus took place that plastered my face and the face of this famous author, Xavier Preston, across TV stations and print media, I did something I never thought I would ever do. I had plastic surgery. Nothing too major or extreme, à la Michael Jackson. Just a few tweaks here and there, mainly on my face. It was enough to make me unrecognizable to the general public.

Add some gray contact lenses to the equation, along with coloring, relaxing, and straightening my naturally curly hair. Then throw in a few extra pounds, and I was no longer the person the entire nation saw splashed across their TV screens for weeks. I could come and go freely without the scrutiny of finger-pointing, stares, and frowns. I had even changed my last name; I couldn't resist the urge to keep my first name. So, I was still Pilar. I would always be Pilar and everything that it stood for.

As the wheels of the plane touched down on the runway, I was literally beaming. I was sure happiness from within was radiating outward for all to see. I was back. And Xavier had better watch his back, because this time I was bringing it. Last time was just child's play.

Chapter 6

Dre'

The professional men and women of Houston were slowly, but surely, spilling into the trendy restaurant and after-hours bar. It was the newest hot spot at the moment. Most were still dressed in their business attire, myself included. We all desired the same thing: to unwind, de-stress, and begin our weekend with a good time.

As usual, the women outnumbered the men. I didn't think I would trade living in Houston with any other major city in the country, with the exception of perhaps Atlanta. A man like me could get seriously spoiled rotten here.

What I mean by "a man like me" is that after two unsuccessful marriages, I was no longer looking for love. What the hell was love? I wasn't even sure I believed it existed anymore. It was similar to no longer believing in the Easter Bunny or Santa Claus as a kid.

Two times I thought I was in love, head over heels, and within a few years, the illusions faded, and all I was left with was two angry bitches. Women were like vampires. They sucked, sucked, and sucked, until they'd sucked all the life out of a man. And then they still weren't satisfied. Houston women were notorious gold diggers. Always had their hands out, palm up and wide open, waiting for some man to take care of all their needs. Well, I wasn't the one. Not anymore. Been there. Done that. End of story.

Don't get me wrong. There were many professional, highly intelligent, independent, successful women who had it all. Superwomen. I worked with some. At the end of the day, the money they made on their own was their money; they desired our money to satisfy their wants.

Personally, regardless of what my ex-wives thought, I realized I was a good catch. Hell, I had a well-paying job with many perks as a vice president of a major financial institution. I had made some good investments, even in this recession, and I owned a home and two nice luxury cars. Hell yeah, I had it going on. With my bald head and goatee, my smooth brown skin, women always commented that I resembled that famous black chef G. Garvin. I could afford to lose maybe ten pounds, but other than that I was the man.

I took my time with my drink as I sat at the L-shaped bar and eavesdropped on lively conversations on either side of me. I had a group of beautiful women to my left and a couple of attractive girlfriends to my right. I wasn't in a hurry, and I was in a mellow mood. It was a Friday evening, the night was still young, and I didn't have any specific plans for the weekend ahead.

"Girl, I finally had the opportunity to check out that movie, *Diary of a Stalker,* that you've been raving about for weeks now." This was coming from one of the women sitting to my right, who was dressed in a black skirt, a blouse, and sexy, come-fuck-me shoes.

"I'm glad, because you are about the only person I know who hadn't seen it. I'm glad you finally decided to check it out," her slightly overweight girlfriend with the honey blond locks stated matter-of-factly.

They paused long enough to take sips of their colorful drinks before continuing.

"Well, don't keep me in suspense. What did you think?" Locks asked.

"Girl, I was absolutely blown away. I loved it! That Pilar was a true beast."

"Tell me about it. You hated her and loved her all rolled into one. She was most definitely one not to be played with."

"I felt bad about some of the abuse she suffered through as a child," Black Skirt stated. "That broke my heart."

Locks agreed by nodding.

"Our childhoods really do shape who we eventually become. Some of us have fucked-up childhoods and end up fucked up as adults, too. Others overcome and move forward with a vengeance."

"I guess you are right. But, yeah, I felt sorry for her at times, too," Locks said, genuinely looking sad, as if she was about to cry in a few seconds. "Girl, what did you think about that sexy-ass Xavier?" Locks asked a moment later, throwing her hand up toward the heavens.

"Wasn't he as fine as hell? Ain't nothing like those tall, dark, and sexy brothers. Who could ask for more? Lordy, have mercy, Jesus," Black Skirt cried out. "He could hit this any day," she added.

I had the opportunity to check her out from the corner of my eye. She was the type of woman that made me instantly hard. I loved asses—big ones—and thighs on my woman, and Black Skirt had an ample supply of both. The way her cheeks took over that bar stool told it all. I could picture her legs wrapped tightly around my waist as I pounded in and out with no mercy.

"I have heard so many women say he deserved exactly what he received and then some. Pilar showed his ass exactly who he was messing with. Damn, Pilar was bad. I bet he would think twice about who he brought into his bed next time around," Locks stated with a smirk on her face.

As much as I wanted to jump in and defend my man Xavier, I knew from experience that it was a useless fight. Bottom line, people were going to think what they wanted to. Everyone had an opinion. It also amazed me how women talked graphically to one another when they thought no one was listening. I insisted on my woman having class in public, but behind closed doors it was on. I loved to hear her talk dirty as I gave it back even stronger.

Skirt surprised me with her next comment.

"I don't know if I agree with that. Xavier was simply being a man. Sure, he was thinking with the wrong head, like most men, but I will give him credit. He did inform Pilar up front, on more than one occasion, that he was only in it for the sex."

"He did, true, but then he kept coming back for more—got greedy with it. What's up with that? He had a beautiful fiancée at home, and yet he was out and about, screwing around," Locks stated, with a scowl on her face, as she played with her long locks between sips of her drink.

"He hadn't learned a simple lesson. In most cases, you can't have your cake and eat it, too." This was said by Black Skirt.

"Well, he could have all my cake and the frosting and come back for second helpings." Locks laughed, looking down at herself and taking a few more sips of her drink. "In fact, I'd love for him to lick the frosting."

"I heard this was based on a true story," Skirt stated, bopping her head to the music of the live band that had started its set in another section of the restaurant.

"Yeah. You don't remember this story from a few years ago, when that author was plastered all over the

TV for assaulting some chick he claimed was stalking him? Well, this is what the movie is based upon."

"Oh yeah, I do kind of remember it now. I had just moved to Houston, but it made national headlines because of his celebrity status," Black Skirt replied. "I wonder if he still lives in the area."

That was my cue. It was perfect timing, because I had just finished my drink and I was tired of pretending not to listen to them.

"Indeed he does," I stated, looking directly at Black Skirt. I nodded at Locks.

Black Skirt smiled, and in the few seconds it took for her to respond, she sized me up completely, from my expensive suit to my watch and shoes. Locks played the role of not being interested.

"And how would you know that?" Black Skirt asked, licking her glossy lips.

"And why are you all in our conversation?" Locks questioned.

"Let me buy you and your friend another round of drinks, and I'll tell you the entire story. By the way, my name is Dre'," I stated, more to Black Skirt.

"I'm Jennifer, and this is my friend Lisa," she replied, reaching to shake hands.

They agreed to the drinks, and I knew without a shadow of a doubt that I'd be between those thick thighs before the night was over. If I had been paying more attention to my surroundings, to something besides the two attractive women in front of me, I would have noticed a mysterious woman intensely checking me out, watching my every move. Much like a wild animal stalking her prey.

Chapter 7

Xavier

I still could not conceive of the whirlwind year I had somehow survived and conquered. Living out in la-la land and watching my vision get turned into a movie right before my eyes, witnessing the reactions as moviegoers and critics embraced it all across the country, yes, the last year of my life on some levels had been phenomenal. It was what every writer dreamt of.

There was one small, well, actually, rather large blemish, which stole the joy away. All my success had come from the unfortunate circumstances that resulted from dealing with psycho Pilar. It all began and ended with her. While out in L.A. I kept busy with completing the movie project, being an executive producer, networking, making important contacts, doing power lunches, and meeting new and exciting people, including one in particular who took care of my needs on the regular. I was never really alone, never had the opportunity to seriously focus on Pilar and what had occurred between us. Sure, it was in my face every day, what with the movie; however, soon it became just that—a movie. I was watching actors and actresses do what they did best, act. That wasn't about my life. At least I told myself that when my thoughts became too overwhelming.

Now that I was home, in Houston, with lots of time on my hands, I didn't know what to do with myself. I had originally planned to take a year off, to enjoy my successes and money, and not leap back into writing anything new so quickly. I realized I was burned out both physically and mentally. Not writing lasted only a few weeks, as I became stir-crazy living in my large home, alone with my random thoughts, which, one way or another, always drifted back to Pilar.

"Hey, babe. Are you okay?" Bailey asked, looking at me strangely.

We were sitting in my spacious living room, cuddled up under a warm blanket, watching a mystery thriller she had chosen earlier.

"I thought I told you not to call me that," I said, massaging my forehead and sighing.

"Call you what?"

"Babe," I said quietly. That was the term of endearment Pilar had always used when referring to me. Now I despised it with a passion.

"Okay, sweetie. I'm sorry. Dang," she stated, snuggling closer to me, if that was humanly possible.

I didn't comment one way or the other.

"Are you enjoying the movie?" she asked, looking up at me and frowning. "You appear to be distracted. Something on your mind?"

"The movie is all right. I was just lost in my random thoughts for a minute."

Bailey pouted like a child. It was times like this when the age difference between us was apparent and I wondered if she was worth the drama.

"Xavier, I didn't fly all the way from L.A. for you to be into your thoughts. I want you to be into me, sweetie."

"Well, it wasn't like I was expecting you. You did show up unannounced."

She looked hurt and pouted even more, looking like the young woman she was.

"I'm sorry, Bailey. For the rest of the night, I am all yours, baby." I nuzzled her neck. "Okay? You forgive me?"

"Okay," she said and smiled, subtly rubbing her breasts against my arm.

She appeared pleased with my apology, and we resumed watching the movie she had picked out at the local Blockbuster after we finished dinner at one of my favorite seafood restaurants downtown.

Bailey had wanted to go clubbing, but I wasn't up for that. I desired a quiet night at home, and that was exactly what was happening now. I couldn't believe it was almost the end of February already. I had lit a cozy fire in the fireplace, popped buttered popcorn, and now Bailey and I were hugged up like a couple.

A couple.

That thought disturbed me on many levels. It made me uneasy. My attention turned from the movie to Bailey. Sure, she was a gorgeous woman; no one could deny that. She was rather young, only twenty-five, but when I first met her on the set of the stalker movie, she reminded me of a younger version of Kendall, my ex-fiancée.

By day and into the late evenings, Bailey was one of the production assistants, but by night we screwed like we invented sex. I fucked her like it was going out of style. I fucked her every which way but loose. I made a point to inform her up front that it was what it was. We were friends with benefits. I wasn't looking for a relationship.

Bailey appeared to be cool with that *each* time I reminded her as she left my bed. I knew that sounded mean and cruel, like I was simply using her for sex, but

I didn't want any confusion like the last time. So, I laid it on the table. That way there would be no surprises down the line. On some level, I probably did use her like she was my personal sex toy. However, I never heard any complaints from her, because the moans were too loud as she was being thoroughly satisfied, if I must say so myself. Through sex, I was able to pound out all the frustration I was trying to suppress.

When I left L.A., I had no intention of ever seeing her again—out of sight, out of mind. That was a motto I lived by. It worked for me. But after receiving a call from out of the blue that she was in the city, here we were, snuggled up like a couple. That didn't sit well with me at all. Again, I wasn't looking for a relationship now or in the near future. Kendall and Pilar had made me rethink relationships, both in different ways.

Bailey glanced up at me, smiled, and readjusted her position on the sofa. She was now leaning her head on my shoulder and had her arms wrapped snugly across my chest. I had seen this all before. Been there, done that. She was starting to think of us as a couple.

Suddenly she sat up and proceeded to slowly unbutton her blouse, teasing me in the process, to reveal a fire red, lacy bra. Her breasts were at eye level and almost screamed for me to reach out and pluck them.

"You like what you see?" she asked seductively, licking her lips.

"I love what I see," I stated.

"I can tell," she giggled, reaching out to massage my semi-erect penis through my pants.

"Touch me, sweetie, while we watch the rest of the movie. We can pretend we are making out on your parents' sofa like teenagers." I thought to myself, it had been many years since I was petting on my mama's sofa.

Bailey turned her attention back to the movie, but as her chest heaved up and down and her breathing changed, I knew she was already hot. Bailey enjoyed sex, and I had no qualms with that.

I slowly lifted her bra up and out of my way. Her ample, firm breasts spilled forward instantly. I admired them for a few seconds, because I was definitely a breast man. I proceeded to tweak her nipples between my thumb and finger, watching as they swelled and became firm and taut. She involuntarily arched her back, which pushed her breasts forward and out.

"Oh, babe, I mean sweetie, that feels so good when you stroke me like that," she purred into my ear. "Don't stop."

I bent my head to suckle a nipple, one, then the other, over and over again. Once more she moaned, but she continued to pretend to watch the movie. My tongue flickered across her nipples again. Now she had my nature fully alert and ready to play. She reached down to squeeze and tease me.

"Take your top off," I demanded.

She readily compiled as I watched in desire.

"Your pants and thong, too."

She delivered a sly smile but did as requested. She took her time undressing because she knew I enjoyed it that way, revealing herself to me a little at a time. When she bent down to step out of her clothes, her round ass was turned smack in my face, only inches away.

I ran my large hand across it, caressing it. "You have a beautiful body."

"Thank you. Now, do what you do so wonderfully, sweetie," she said, standing before me completely nude, and not embarrassed to show me what she was working with, even though I already knew from being inside her numerous times.

My eyes were lust filled. "Come here," I said, reaching for her hand to pull her into my lap, with her facing the TV. "Wait a minute," I said, pushing her back up. I took a few moments to unbuckle my belt and pull my pants down to my ankles. "Now we're set. Sit your pretty ass down." I moaned.

"Ahhh, sweetie, are you happy to see me?" she joked.

"You are going to find out in just a few seconds how happy I am. Watch the movie, and don't worry about what I'm doing."

"Are you going to make my kitty purr?" she teased, licking her lips seductively.

"Don't I always?" I said with a confident, almost arrogant air. If there were two things I knew about myself, they were that I could write my ass off and I could set a woman's pussy on fire. Bailey was no exception; within minutes she would be coming like a raging, flowing river. Totally dick whipped.

With her straddling my lap, I went back to fondling her breasts and maneuvering my fingers into the space between her thighs.

"Open up your legs," I demanded.

She obliged and enjoyed the fact that I was an aggressive lover. I didn't have any time for those shy chicks. When it came to sex, either you came ready to ride, or you had better get off the horse.

"Wider, baby, for Daddy."

I ran a finger over her clit, and she jumped like an electric shock had penetrated her within.

"Why are you so wet? Are you hot for me?"

"Damn right."

I stuck another finger in, even deeper, and burrowed my face firmly into her back. Soon I was in a smooth rhythm of finger penetration and tweaking her tantalizing nipples.

Bailey looked back, reaching for my cheek, with lust-filled eyes that spoke of burning desire.

"Don't look at me. Watch the movie," I teased, spreading her legs wide open.

"Damn, sweetie, you have me feeling so good right now," she moaned, moving into a natural groove with my fingers. Once again, she reached back to stroke my cheek. "Ahhh, sweetie, you're the best."

"Get up for a minute," I suddenly stated, as I moved so that I was reclining on my back on the sofa.

She stood.

"Come here," I said, pulling her backward so I could rub my hand across her firm buttocks. I slapped them a couple of times and left red marks. She sucked up the sudden pain and moaned loudly. "Sit that sweet ass on my face."

Looking at me in anticipation, Bailey compiled with my wishes.

"Now, watch the movie, Bailey!"

I lifted her a bit, pulled her wide open, and inserted a finger; then my wet tongue followed. Bailey was already trembling, and her legs were shaking involuntarily in anticipation.

"Yes, sweetie! Eat that shit out! It's all yours!"

I proceeded to do just that. I had to force her to remain steady on my face. My oral skills were so on point that she kept trying to get away because she couldn't take the good feelings it generated.

"Sweetie, I'm about to come," she screamed. "Damn, ooh, damn, that feels so good. So muthafucking good. Don't you dare stop."

"Yes, yes, right there. Oooh, that's it. Get it, sweetie!" she yelled. "Ahhh, I'm coming!"

Just as the movie ended, Bailey let out an unearthly, primal scream and came in my mouth. As she lowered herself, or more like slid her nude body to the floor beside the sofa, she looked back at me with a sexy smile, and it was then that I saw that look in her eyes . . . One I had seen before. She was totally caught up!

I dismissed the thought for the moment because my dick was ready to be taken care of. I gently reached for her hand. "Let's take this upstairs and finish what we've started."

"Sounds good to me."

"Are you ready to suck some dick?"

She eagerly nodded. Unlike Kendall, my ex-fiancée, Bailey was anxious to please.

"Good girl," I said as I slapped her ass a couple of times and led the way.

A couple of hours later, totally sated from our earlier efforts, I woke Bailey to drive her back to her hotel.

"Bailey, wake up," I whispered as I slipped into my underwear and pants from the floor on my side of the bed.

"Nooo, sweetie. I'm tired. Let me sleep. You wore me out," she said, barely opening an eye, reaching for me.

"No, Bailey. Get up. Get dressed. You know our agreement. I need to take you back to your room."

"Let's break it this one time. Okay?" she asked sleepily.

"Come on. Get up," I said, more forcefully this time, snatching the light sheet from around her nude body.

That got her attention, and she turned to glare at me.

"Damn it, Xavier! Quit being so fucking mean."

Picking up her cell phone from the nightstand, squinting to glare at the screen, she said, "It is four o'clock in the morning. It would not kill you if I spent the night this one time. Damn, man. What is your freaking problem?"

"You know my rule. I explained it at the very beginning of our relationship. I don't spend the night, and my lovers don't stay over, either. That's the agreement."

"Well, I'm not feeling our agreement. I thought by now I would be an exception and would be more than just a lover. I flew all the way from California to be with your ass, and now, after fucking me, you are putting me out?" She scowled. "Unbelievable."

"I'm not putting you out. I told you I'm going to drive you back to your warm, cozy hotel room, and you can go right back to sleep."

"Same thing."

"Whatever, Bailey."

"Yeah, whatever!" she screamed, tossing a pillow in my face as she frantically searched for her discarded clothing.

That pissed me off. It wasn't like she was hearing this for the first time.

"Listen, Bailey, let me make a few things perfectly clear once and for all. Number one, I didn't invite you to come to Houston. You simply showed up. That was your choice, not mine. Number two, not spending the night is one of my rules, and if you don't like it, cannot accept it, then, well, you know what you can do. Number three, you are not an exception. I don't mean to hurt your feelings, but I'm not looking for a relationship right now or anytime in the near future. I have told you this several times, so it shouldn't come as a surprise. And lastly, what we have is strictly sexual. If you can't get with the program, well then . . ."

When I was finished with my tirade, I noticed Bailey wouldn't or couldn't meet my eye, but she did get dressed without uttering another word. When she went to the bathroom, behind closed doors, I heard her softly crying. I continued to dress and pretended not to hear her. I knew my words had sounded cruel, but I had discovered that women would hear what they wanted to. I was determined to never make the same mistakes I had made with Pilar. Never again.

Most of the drive was in silence, with the exception of the Silent Storm tunes that played on the radio and the smooth, sexy voice of the female radio personality that spoke between songs.

I reached over to lightly touch Bailey's thigh. "Are you still mad at me?" I asked and smiled, flashing my dimples and trying to look as sincere as possible. I realized I might have been a little too harsh with her, but I wanted her to realize I was very serious.

She didn't respond, kept staring out the window, into the darkness, as if it fascinated her.

"I really enjoyed myself tonight, and I hope you did, too." As I spoke, my hand inched its way up near the button to her pants.

Bailey didn't respond, but she didn't move my hand away, either. That was a good sign.

"You are a beautiful girl, Bailey, but I'm not searching for a relationship right now. I've had a rough couple of years, and I need to chill for a minute."

"I'm not a girl," she stated, not turning my way. She still continued to look out the window, as if all the answers to life were out there.

As I started to undo her button, I paused for a moment to get her reaction. Bailey didn't resist me. I took that as my signal to continue.

"I'm sorry. You are definitely a woman, and a man would be blind not to see that." With my hand, I massaged her womanhood through the fabric of her panties. Firm strokes that heated her up quickly.

"I could be so good for you, Xavier," she moaned.

"You probably could, but I'm not looking for that right now. I like things the way they are, purely sexual. If you can't deal with that . . ."

"Why do you have to be so mean, Xavier?" she asked, still unable to look at me. By now, I had managed to pull her pants and panties down near her ankles. She didn't resist and even lifted herself up to make it easier. Not many people were on the road that early, and besides, it was still dark outside and no one could see what we were up to, or witness my erratic driving.

"Open your legs for me," I said.

Bailey didn't move. She simply pouted.

I turned her face around with my hand, very gently. "You know I can never get enough of you." As I continued to drive, my fingers skillfully and easily slid in and out of her womanhood.

"Why did you treat me like that?" she asked again, squirming in her seat.

"Unbutton your blouse," I said, disregarding her question.

"No, someone may see."

"They won't. I promise. Look around. There is barely anyone on the road."

She slowly unbuttoned her blouse to reveal that she hadn't bothered to put her red, lacy bra back on in her haste to leave.

"I want to make sure you understand where we stand," I said, fondling her freed breasts.

She moaned, and I could tell she was trying with everything in her to keep from enjoying my advances. I dove deeper with my fingers.

"Hmmm, you are so wet. Do you like when I touch you?"

She didn't respond as she bit down on her lower lip and a soft moan escaped.

"Huh? Do you like how I make you flow?"

She still continued to ignore me as I continued to reach for her breasts and stimulate her manually. At a red light, I gave her everything I had, and just as I expected, she couldn't hold back.

"Yeah, that's my girl," I stated, smiling. "Let it go."

"I hate you," she screamed as she came all over my fingers.

"No, you don't. Let it go. That's right."

"Yes, I do," she screamed in between moans. "You don't know how hard I try."

When she was finished, I slowly removed my fingers from inside her warm walls and licked her sticky wetness off. "Didn't that feel good? You know you love it," I said jokingly, running my fingers through her hair.

She slowly redressed and reached to unzip my zipper. Right as she bent to retrieve my dick, I stopped her by gently pulling her head back.

"Bailey, are we on the same page now? I really need to know."

She looked up at me and reluctantly said, "Yeah, Xavier. We are."

I released her, and she proceeded to give me one of the best blow jobs I'd ever had before I dropped her off at the entrance to her hotel and saw her safely in.

After sexing each other on two more occasions, making her stay in Houston memorable, she boarded a plane a day later, totally sated. I couldn't truthfully say I would miss her.

***

The cute young child, who always had a disheveled, not-cared-for appearance, placed her tiny hand over her stomach to stop the growling and nagging hunger pangs that tormented her. She hadn't eaten since lunch on Friday at school. It was now Saturday evening.

Her mother was bent over the hot stove, cigarette dangling precariously from her thin, red-painted lips, frying up some golden brown, crispy, crunchy, delicious-smelling chicken. Her mother hummed an alluring tune about a beautiful woman finding true love and living happily ever after. More growls escaped her tummy, but she knew not to complain.

The young child could barely stop herself from jumping up from the sofa, where she quietly watched TV, and sneaking a piece of chicken from the half-full plate that sat on the countertop. She glanced shyly at her mother without capturing her attention. At times like this, her mother was actually pretty in her eyes. The child knew her mother was pretty, beautiful even, because she was very aware of the fact that men constantly admired her and gave her their time and money. However, her ugly ways overtook any beauty that existed on the surface, and there definitely wasn't any within. That had long ago dissipated, never to be seen again.

Finally, the crispy, golden brown chicken was done and ready to be eaten. She watched anxiously as her mother fixed a plate with a plump drumstick and a wing, then added green beans and brown rice. The *child stood quietly and patiently by to retrieve her own plate and quench the hungriness that had overcome her and made her weak. Her mouth was actually watering over the thought of biting into a piece of the golden goodness.*

"Where the hell do you think you are going?" her mother screamed. It seemed like she was always screaming; she never talked quietly or patiently. She talked sweetly only to the many "uncles" that came and went, as if their apartment was a revolving door to pleasure.

"To fix my plate," the child barely whispered, with her eyes focused on the floor. She rarely looked her mother directly in the eyes. Later in life she would wonder if it was because of fear, or if it was because she didn't want her to see the hatred for her that lived there as a permanent resident.

"Get your ugly ass out of here! I didn't tell you to fix a damn thing. Now, get!" she screamed, pointing a finger. "Get!" she screeched again, like she was shooing a stray dog away.

The child tried hard to control tears that threatened to spill, but sometimes it was just too hard. She knew what followed the tears, usually pain. An hour later, after her mother had feasted and filled her stomach, only then was the child allowed to enter the filthy kitchen and eat the leftovers. That night, she prayed that God would forgive her for whatever she had done wrong in her short time on earth. Only the wrath of God could have sent her as a daughter to this person who called herself her mother.

Chapter 8

Pilar

I managed to duck down in the driver's seat of my car just in the nick of time, when the garage door suddenly and unexpectedly inched slowly upward. He backed out of the driveway and turned his car in my direction. Headlights shone my way. I ducked farther down and prayed I had not been seen. I didn't think so. I had thought for sure they were in for the night, but reminded myself I definitely had to be more careful the next time. There couldn't be any mistakes or close calls.

Mere seconds after the couple drove by, I dared to sneak a quick peek. My heart did a quick pitter-patter and a double somersault. I silently willed myself to calm down. Regardless of all that had happened or had not happened between Xavier and me, I realized I still loved him, probably always would. He was my soul mate, plain and simple. The problem was that he didn't love me back, and that was a big problem. After the way he portrayed me in his movie, I realized he probably hated me just as much as I adored him.

I recalled that initially I was so excited about the movie opening at the box office; I could barely sleep the night before. I tossed and turned for most of it, into the wee morning hours. The movie opened on a Friday. I was there front and center and probably had the best seat in the theater. I had purchased a large popcorn with butter and a Diet Sprite. I was thrilled that the world would finally see and hear *our* story on the big screen. I could barely contain myself as I squirmed, wiggled around in my stadium chair, trying to make it through the trailers of forthcoming movies.

The first time I saw *Diary of a Stalker,* I wanted it to be by myself, so Michael, my boyfriend at the time, didn't come with me. I wanted to absorb the very essence and fiber of the film. Just knowing Xavier had a stake in the making of this production brought me renewed joy. I just knew he would do justice to *our* story. Was I ever wrong.

When the first scene appeared on the big screen, I immediately realized that Xavier's version of *our* story was much different from my version. The longer I sat there and watched, the more my world slowly turned red, nothing but vibrant shades of red, which attested to my fury. I was angry, so mad that I didn't realize I had squeezed the large soda between my hands and had burst the foam cup until I felt the ice-cold liquid running down my lap and thighs. I still didn't move.

I simply sat there. I sat there and saw red and didn't try to clean myself up. I had to witness every detail of the monster he portrayed me to be on the big screen. How dare he! How dare he! How motherfucking dare he!

I wanted to scream this at all the moviegoers, who gasped and shuddered as each scene played out in vibrant Technicolor. Xavier came across smelling like roses, a pure saint, while I became the evil, deranged villain. Hell no. He was not going to get away with this. I refused to bend over and let him stick me yet again. I felt like he had made a mockery of what we once shared. I felt totally betrayed, like he had stuck a knife in my heart and twisted it. No, it wasn't good all the time, but what relationship was?

During the scene where his character was beating the main character that portrayed me, I cried as the audience eagerly cheered his character on. "Yeah, beat her ass!" "Knock some sense into that crazy-ass bitch!" I couldn't believe my ears. I still had not figured out how I managed to see the movie to the end, because I was so mad that my clenched teeth started to hurt my jaw after a while. I wanted to hit something, hurt someone, and the one person that came to mind was Xavier. I was so upset that I accidentally urinated on myself, but I still didn't move one inch, not one. I couldn't miss anything. I was determined to see the on-screen rape and sodomy of the focal points of what he called our dysfunctional affair.

When it was over, I stiffly lifted my body from the seat, brushing the buttered popcorn that had collected on my lap onto the floor. I put my coat on to hide my wetness and blindly followed the crowd out of the theater. I heard the comments and took them all in.

"That Pilar was one crazy bitch!"

"Wow, if I were Xavier, I would have beaten her ass, too. In fact, she got off light."

"She was one sick puppy!"

It took every ounce of energy I could muster to make my way out the exit door. I saw the movie a total of thirty more times, and each and every time I left filled with just as much pain and fury as the first time. I was determined I was going to teach Xavier a lesson, one he wouldn't forget so easily this time. He was one hardheaded mofo, who still hadn't learned not to fuck with me.

I dropped the assault and battery charges against him; I couldn't help it if the state of Texas decided to proceed without me based on the evidence. I had left him alone for two entire years now. Not a single contact was made. I even suffered through letting Michael screw me for a year before I had to teach him a lesson, too. I had thought that during that time Xavier would realize what a true gem he had found in me and that no one would treat him the way I could, no one. I loved him from my soul, as well as from my heart. Now I hated him just as much, and that was not a good thing. Not good for him, anyway.

I watched him drive off with his tramp. There wasn't a need for me to follow them, because I had a pretty good idea where they were headed. I smiled to myself when I thought about how earlier I had trailed Xavier to the hotel to pick her up for dinner. She kind of reminded me of his ex-fiancée. What was her name? Kerr . . . Krystal? No, Kendall. Yeah, that was it. Miss High-and-Mighty Kendall, nose all stuck up in the air. Miss Future Lawyer. Yeah, I fixed her ass, too. I fixed her good. This one, she was young, too. Xavier liked them young so he could train them like little puppies so they could grow up to be his tamed bitches. Well, he couldn't train or tame me. He found that out real quick and in a hurry.

After their fancy dinner, I trailed Xavier and his tramp back to his house. They never spotted me. It was too easy. It always was. I had been sitting out in the cold, in my car, since. I knew all too well what they were doing up in there—what Xavier did best besides writing. Now he was probably taking her back to the hotel. I didn't attempt to follow, because I knew everything I needed to know about her. Miss Bailey. I'd deal with her later. I was finished for the night, but tomorrow was another day.

Just as I was attempting to pull away from the curb, my cell signaled that I had a text. I quickly retrieved it and read:

Pilar, please contact me as soon as possible. I'm worried about you. Please call.

I knew exactly who it was from. I pressed ERASE, more than slightly annoyed now. I had been getting text messages and voice messages since I left Los Angeles behind, which was almost a month ago.

Another text followed.

Have you been taking your meds? I hope so, because you were doing so well. I'm proud of you. Call me. I'm going to wait by the phone in my office a while longer, or call me later on my cell.

My friend Leeda wouldn't leave me alone. Oh, okay, I should call her what she really was. My ex-psychiatrist wouldn't stop harassing me. To be honest, she had been a great friend over the years; I couldn't deny that. I was sure she had heard of Michael's suicide by now. Poor baby. But to my credit, I did contact her. I sent her a text to be exact, to let her know I was leaving L.A. and would be in touch with her soon. I left out the part about first completing my master plan in Houston. She didn't need to know all that, because Leeda was a worrywart and loved to stay all up in my business.

Tomorrow I planned to purchase a new cell phone with a new phone number, which I'd use until my plan was carried out. It shouldn't take too long. Only then would Leeda hear from me again. Not a day sooner.

I smiled as I slowly pulled off, because I was now ready to set the wheels in motion. Xavier had no idea what he was in store for.

Chapter 9

Dre'

Holding up my empty glass, I caught the bartender's attention. "Give me another round, man."

As the twenty-something African American male mixed my Bacardi and Coke, I turned and surveyed the enormous room. It was eye-catching with its sleek, clean, and sexy modern design. The usual crowd was not out in force this evening, unlike two Fridays ago, when it was standing room only. I assumed many of the regular patrons had made plans to attend the Maxwell and Jill Scott concert, which was the talk of the town.

I reached for my drink, which the bartender had placed in front of me, on a white napkin, and took a big gulp. This workweek had been a killer, and I needed a weekend break, preferably with a fine female companion, to recoup. However, I noticed the few women at the bar were coupled up, and as I glanced around, no one in particular caught my eye, anyway. I realized the evening was still young, and I intended to hang out a bit longer.

I pulled out my cell, dialed the familiar digits, and listened to it ring a couple of times.

"Hello."

"What's up, man?" I asked.

"Nothing much. What you getting into tonight?"

"I'm here at the spot."

"You getting started early, aren't you?" Xavier asked.

"Man, it's the weekend, and it couldn't have come any sooner. I've told you that all of us normal, ordinary people aren't fortunate enough to work from home and pen tall tales." I laughed good-humoredly, taking another gulp of my drink and relishing the mellow mood it was putting me in. My job was a high-pressure one, and at times like this, I simply needed to relax and regroup.

"Dre', you know you are closing million-dollar deals and bringing home big-ass commission checks. Who are you fooling? That shit makes your dick hard, and you wouldn't trade it for the world."

"What can I say?" I laughed again. "Your pretty young thing still got you hemmed up?"

Xavier chuckled. "No, I put her on a plane last night, but I think she is still a little pissed."

"Why? I figured she would leave with a big smile on her face."

"Dre', you stupid man." He laughed.

"I'm just glad you came to your senses and are getting back out there."

"I was never gone, man. Besides, I fooled around with Bailey out in L.A. She was something to do, and hanging with her made the time go by quicker."

"You could have fooled me, because when you first came back to Houston, I was worried about your ass for a minute."

"Why?"

"Because you were all hemmed in at your house, acting like you were afraid to venture outside and be seen in public."

There was a telling silence.

"You there?" I asked.

"Yeah, I'm here. There may be some truth to that. I was in a bad place. There is no doubt about that."

"Damn, man. Forget about that psycho once and for all."

"It's not as easy as it sounds, but I'm coming out of it. Better days are ahead. I can feel it."

"On a serious tip, do you think you should talk to someone about what happened?" I asked, bracing for his response as I scoped out the new crowd of beautiful women who had entered the building.

"I know you aren't talking about a shrink."

"Yes."

"Dre', I'm not that far gone. It's just different. It's hard to explain. . . . It's difficult being back here because this is where it all went down. Believe it or not, I know you and I joke around about a lot of it, but it was a traumatic experience. I'm not going to lie. I'm adjusting day by day, and it's not going to happen overnight."

"I know I kid around a lot. That's just me. But I'm here for you. Got your back. Always will."

"I know that, and I appreciate it, Dre'."

"What's up with baby girl? Why her drawers in a bunch, or does she wear any? Why she pissed off at you?"

"Bailey is trying her best to inch her way into a relationship, and I'm not having it. No way, no how."

"What's the deal with all these desperate women you attract?"

"Who you asking?"

"Did you hurt baby girl's feelings?"

"No, not intentionally. I enforced some ground rules, and evidently, that didn't sit well with her."

"Do what you have to do, man. I'm not mad at ya. You are definitely going to have every gold-digging chick out there trying to hook up with you now, palms wide open. If you thought you could get the drawers before, you haven't seen anything yet. Didn't I tell you about the two women I met here two weeks ago? They were seriously into you. Talking about having your babies and picking out china patterns."

Xavier laughed. "Yeah, you told me. You also informed me how you turned the tables and used our friendship to your advantage."

"Ain't no shame in my game. Besides, I didn't lie, and it worked. I hit it until the early morning hours."

"Well, personally, I'm not going through what I went through with Pilar ever again. Even though I still don't feel I sent mixed signals, from this point on, I'm going to make my intentions very clear with every female I date. If their feelings get hurt in the breakdown, then they need to step if they can't handle the truth."

"I hear you, my brotha. Just make sure you do it after you hit it, and then you can quit it," I suggested, downing the last of my drink.

"Man, just handle your own business. Don't worry about mine."

"I intend to do just that," I declared as a brown beauty slowly walked my way, making intense eye contact. I flashed a smile and quickly hung up with Xavier. It looked like the evening was going to be interesting, after all. In the time it took her to cross the room and arrive by my side at the bar, I decided that there was something familiar about her. I felt like I had seen her or met her before. I couldn't put my finger on where, though.

When she strolled up beside me, with whatever intoxicating fragrance she was wearing, and I realized she was even more beautiful up close, all thoughts except getting with her went out the door.

Then she looked over at me with beautiful, expressive eyes, smiled, and said in a sexy tone, "Hi. My name is Milan."

"And I'm Dre'," I stated, extending my hand. "Milan, what a beautiful name for a gorgeous lady." I swear to you when our hands touched, electricity ignited, and I knew I was in for an adventure. Just like that, I was pulled in.

In hindsight, I realized I should have listened to my first instinct, that inner voice whispering in my head. But I guess that's why it's called hindsight, because at that moment I was feeling no pain.

Chapter 10

Xavier

After hanging up with Dre', I couldn't do anything but shake my head and laugh out loud. He was quite the character, and I loved him like a blood brother. I didn't know why I had never written about him in one of my novels, changing the name, of course. Hell, he would make a great character, but I knew the answer to that question already. I realized Dre' was the keeper of too many of my own secrets, which he might be inclined to reveal were I to offer revelations about him. I'm not going to lie. Back in the day, I was no joke. Neither one of us was. Dre' and I sowed enough wild oats to last two lifetimes each.

After working out like a madman for a solid two hours in my home gym, I had worked up quite a sweat. I wandered upstairs to the kitchen and drank another eight ounces of bottled water, leaning on the granite island. For the life of me, I didn't know what I would do with myself for the remainder of the night.

If I was honest with myself, I had to admit I did enjoy having a steady woman in my life. It was the staying faithful part that always messed me up, no matter what good intentions I started off with. I thought about Kendall, my ex-fiancée. In fact, I had been thinking of her a lot lately. I didn't know why. Well, yes, I did. I was casually flipping through the pages of *Jet* magazine in the checkout lane of the grocery store a few weeks ago, waiting my turn. And lo and behold, there she was staring back at me, larger than life, in the society column of the magazine. She was as beautiful as I remembered, if not more so. Kendall appeared to be happy, glowing even. The article spoke of her marriage to a prominent Houston surgeon. Apparently, they had had a lavish wedding ceremony, for which the guest list was a who's who of Houston, and then had honeymooned for a month in Paris. I recalled how she and I had spoken of traveling to Europe on many occasions. Due to my busy tour schedule and her classes, we never made it. It was something we were going to do once our lives settled down.

If I had never met Pilar, that could have been us. It's funny how life can throw some serious detours your way that send your life spiraling in a totally different direction. During my grim reflections, my cell vibrated and bounced left and right, like it was having spasms, across the countertop, where I had placed it earlier.

"Hello."

"Hey, sweetie! Whatcha doing?"

"What's up, Bailey? I see you are safe and sound back in la-la land."

"Oh, now you ask. You didn't seem concerned earlier, because you sure didn't phone to check on my safe arrival." I could hear the sassy attitude already saturating the phone.

I thought, *Oh God, here we go.* Why was it that whenever you gave a woman some good dick, suddenly she became super possessive and obsessive?

"I'm sorry, baby. I meant to call, but I lay down to take a short nap after I dropped you off at the airport, and before I realized it, I was knocked out and it was this morning. I figured no news was good news. You can handle yourself."

"Uh-huh," she said, sucking her teeth.

"It's your fault. You wore me out," I said to inject some humor into the conversation.

"Blame it on me."

"You did my little nymph."

"What time is it there? You're not out on the town?" she asked, changing the subject.

"Nope. I just finished my workout. Trying to get back into my regular fitness routine."

"I hear you. You must keep that fine body of yours looking good for all your admirers," she stated sarcastically.

"You seem to like it, because I didn't hear any complaints on your end. In fact, you couldn't get enough," I teased back.

I could almost see the huge smile that lit up her face.

"We did have a good time. You and I are so good together, Xavier. Don't you think?"

"If you say so."

"Oh, it's like that. Thanks, Xavier."

"Bailey, I don't know what else to tell you. I'm not looking—"

"For a relationship," she said, finishing my sentence for me. "I've heard that shit for an entire year now. It's old news."

"Get used to it, because it's the truth and it's not going to change."

"I understand I have no choice, and I simply enjoy hanging out with you, sweetie."

"That's cool. Same here, Bailey."

"I have my last few days of freedom for a while coming up before we start shooting our next movie project. You know how long those days can be. Wouldn't you like for me to come back to Houston and hang out with you? You never showed me around the city. We always managed to wind up in bed. Imagine that."

"That's fine, as long as there aren't any expectations."

"There aren't. I just want to chill, have a good time, and screw you senseless. Know what I mean?" she kidded.

"Well, since you put it like that. Sounds good to me."

"Okay, sweetie. I'll let you know the details later."

"Cool."

"Okay, bye, love."

"Wait. Bailey?"

"Yes?"

"Make sure you make reservations at a hotel close by."

"But I thought—"

"I can send you suggestions if you'd like."

"Don't worry. I can find one myself. I wouldn't want to rain on your parade by staying with you."

With that she hung up, but I had no doubt I would see her soon. And just as quickly she was an afterthought.

"Baby, wake up," the mother said, gently lifting the child from underneath the warm blanket and into her arms.

The young child wiped the sleep from her eyes with the back of her tiny hand and yawned loudly. She looked around, unsure of her surroundings.

Then she remembered she was still at Uncle Danny's house. She had fallen asleep on the sofa in the living room while her mother and Uncle Danny went into his bedroom and closed the door. That was a long time ago.

"Come on, baby." She loved when her mother talked nice to her, which was rare, and called her baby. Those were the few times she felt special and not invisible. She wrapped her arms tighter around her mother's neck.

"Are we leaving?" she asked innocently. It was now after midnight on a school night. She should have long been home, safe and sound in her own bed.

"No. Just be quiet, and be a good girl for me," her mother whispered, like they were playing a game.

"Okay, Mama."

"Just do what he says, and be a good girl."

The young girl's eyes stretched as big as saucers when they entered the musty bedroom of Uncle Danny. To her surprise, he was buck naked, lying on his back, and she saw his thingy, which he didn't even attempt to hide. She looked to her mother for assurance, but her mother averted her eyes. Her mother placed the child in the middle of the bed, disrobed, and *slipped beneath the sheets as if it was as normal as brushing her teeth.*

Right before the young child went to her special place, the one in her mind, she heard her mother say, "Now, you can have both of us. Two for one. Tonight is your lucky night."

That made Uncle Danny very happy, because he smiled and showed every rotten tooth in his mouth.

Chapter 11

Pilar

"Dre', how sweet of you to call. Yes, thank you. I enjoyed talking to you as well the other night. That was crazy. I still can't believe we talked for so long. Three hours. I've never done that before."

"Dinner? This weekend? Sure, I would love to. Let's see. Today is Tuesday, and I'm going to be out of town until Sunday. Okay, Sunday, it is."

"Can't wait, either. Take care."

With a huge grin on my face, I ended the call on my cell. I just loved, loved, loved it when a plan came together so quickly, smoothly, and most of all, effortlessly. I met Dre' last Friday, and I had predicted I would hear from him by today. He didn't disappoint. Men were so predictable. That was the one thing I loved about them. Beyond that, I couldn't think of too much more.

Unbeknownst to Dre', our meeting at the bar was not accidental, as I'd led him to believe. Mostly everything I did in life had some motive behind it, and our little meeting at the bar was no exception. Even though we had never officially been introduced before our "accidental" hookup, I knew of Dre'. I knew all about him being the best friend and confidant of Xavier Preston. I could barely wait; I was going to have some fun with his ass. By the time I was finished with Dre', he would regret the day he spoke to me and offered to buy drinks.

It was actually quite funny. I have always said that people never realized what creatures of routine they truly were. I had been back in Houston for almost two months now. Luckily for me, I already knew the city pretty well due to my past history. As soon as I was situated in my small apartment, not too far from Xavier's house, I went to work with a vengeance, literally. Step one had been completed; I could check it off my list.

I had found that it also paid to know people who had connections, good and bad ones. Money always talked, and I was fortunate to have a trust fund that enabled me to work only if I desired. For now, I was taking a mini-vacation from freelance writing until I saw my plan through to completion. My contact had supplied me with everything I needed, from a fake license to a birth certificate and a Social Security card. Dre' knew me as Milan. And all my documents backed me up. I chose that name because I thought it sounded exotic and exciting.

God, you had to absolutely love technology. I was able to listen to Xavier's phone calls, access his voice mail, and pretty much keep track of his comings and goings through surveillance equipment with him not having a clue. It didn't take too much for my connection to enter Xavier's home and discreetly place spyware throughout. He had even made a house key for me in the process, had thrown it in as an extra, hadn't charged me a dime.

Xavier thought he was safe with his state-of-the-art security system, trying to keep out the bogeyman. I had learned a long time ago that nothing could keep out the bogeyman if he or *she* really wanted to get in. After the way he portrayed me in his damn movie, he had better look under his bed and in his closet every damn night. By the time I was finished with him, he would have to sleep with a night-light and stash a loaded pistol under his down-filled feather pillow.

I flashed back to how easy it had been to meet Dre'. I had followed him for three weeks, and he didn't even realize it. They never did. It was too easy. I knew where he worked, where he lived, and, of course, where he partied. Between him and Xavier, they were my full-time job, which I took seriously. I pretty much memorized their daily routines, which they rarely varied.

As for Xavier, I had immediate plans to deal with his friend with benefits—the slut. The things she let that man do to her. I knew exactly what they did because of the camera in his bedroom. But then again, that was Xavier's MO. He could talk a good game and a woman into doing almost anything for him. As I made the drive to the airport, I couldn't wait to get out to L.A. and handle that bitch. Bailey was her name. Since I had plenty of time before my flight, I wasn't in a hurry to get to the busy airport.

As I drove, my mind quickly slipped back to last Friday at the bar.

"Let me buy that for you. What are you drinking this evening?"

"Cosmo," I stated, *my eyes never leaving his.*

"Cool. Bartender, one Cosmo for the lovely lady."

"Thank you."

"You are most welcome."

The bartender mixed the drink and slid it in my direction, and I picked it up to take a long, slow sip from my tiny plastic straw.

"Hmmm. That hits the spot. Just what the doctor ordered," I sighed.

"Long day?" Dre' asked.

"That's putting it mildly, but I'm happy it's the weekend. I need a few days off to relax and unwind."

"I was just telling my partner the exact same thing. I work hard during the week, but I live for the weekends."

"I hear you," I said and smiled sweetly.

"Why haven't I seen you in here before? I'm pretty much a regular myself," Dre' said, looking at me curiously.

"I'm new to Houston. Moved here from Charlotte, North Carolina, a few weeks ago."

"Oh, that explains it, because I knew I would never overlook a gorgeous face like yours."

I smiled. "Why do you keep staring at me?"

"Something about you feels so familiar, but I can't place my finger on it."

"Really? I hear that all the time." I took another sip, glanced around at the small crowd, checking out the different cliques, and looked back at Dre'.

"You have a beautiful smile. You know that?"

"Well, I've been told," I replied, flirting back.

"What brings you to Houston? Let me guess. Either a man or a job."

"It's definitely not a man."

"Why do you say that with such emotion?"

"I got out of a bad relationship a few months ago."

"Well, we aren't all bad apples."

"Okay, if you say so."

"I heard that."

"I'm a regional sales representative for a pharmaceutical company."

"That sounds like a cool job to have. I guess you travel quite a bit."

"You got it. Sometimes too much for my taste, but it comes with the territory. What field are you in?"

"I'm a vice president at one of the local national banks."

"Sounds intense."

"It can be. I'm an investment banker."

"Wow. Impressive."

"It's a job, nothing special. It pays the bills. Keeps my lights on."

"Stop being so modest. From the looks of you, you are doing quite well for yourself. You must be quite successful."

"I'm not going to lie. I'm good at what I do. . . . I'm one of the best, and being the best has its rewards."

"I bet it does."

And just like that, the conversation took off at lightning speed. I was surprised at how comfortable I felt talking with Dre', and before we realized it, they were locking the doors for the night and literally putting us out. Dre' walked me to my car, arm in arm, and we exchanged phone numbers. Well, I gave him my number. Didn't need his, because I knew I would hear from him again before the week was over. He delivered and didn't disappoint. I could scratch that task off my to-do list.

Chapter 12

Dre'

I disconnected the call and pumped my fist in the air twice for good measure. Like in the old-school Ice Cube song, today was a good day. I was close to signing a new client at the bank, and now, as icing on the cake, Milan had agreed to have dinner with me.

I couldn't stop cheesing, and for some unknown reason, I felt a strong desire to share my good fortune with someone. Xavier immediately came to mind.

I glanced at my watch. It was almost four o'clock, and I knew he had this thing about people calling him when he was writing, but hell, I had to share my news before I burst. I was like a fat kid with cake. It had been a long time since a woman made an impression on me. Usually they were a dime a dozen.

The phone rang and rang, and I was getting ready to hang up when Xavier finally picked up.

"What's up, man?" I asked. "I didn't catch you at a bad time, did I?"

"No, if that's a translation for 'Am I'm writing?' then the answer is that I'm not. I kicked off early today."

"Good for you."

"Why? What's up?"

"Nothing much."

"Dre', man, what's going on? You have never called me in the middle of the day to say hello."

"Okay, you got me. I met this chick."

"And you meet women all the time. We both do."

"This one is different."

"That's what you said about your last two ex-wives."

"Oh, you got jokes today?"

Xavier chuckled. "I'm just saying. Okay, Dre', what makes this woman so special? Educate me."

"I can't explain it myself, but I get this feeling about her when we talk. She's different."

"If you say so, man. Where did you meet her?"

"At the bar. I'm taking her out to dinner Sunday, and I'm really looking forward to it."

"Hmmm."

"Man, you should see her. She's beautiful, with medium-length brown hair, gorgeous eyes, pretty brown skin, and a gorgeous smile. And she has a body to complement it all off."

"You just described a lot of women in Houston."

"Don't rain on my parade."

"You are so serious about this chick you just met a minute ago that you'll get an attitude with me?" Xavier kidded.

"I simply want to see where it will go. I'm not trying to make her wifey number three, or no shit like that. Like I said, we talked for hours and hours, really connected, and that hasn't happened in quite a while. You know me, man. Twenty minutes after meeting a woman, I'm ready to take her back to the crib, knock some boots, and then lose her number."

"I hear you. Just slow your roll, player. Okay? That's all I'm saying."

"I will."

Xavier was silent for a few seconds, as if allowing his advice to sink in.

"I'm listening. I hear you, my brotha," I volunteered.

If only I had really been listening.

Chapter 13

Xavier

"Babe, I've missed you so much. Tell me, did you miss me?" she whispered seductively in my ear as she gently caressed my cheek with her delicate, warm hand. Her touch was light as a feather, and her scent was intoxicating to my senses. She had my head spinning.

"But no, you had to go and fuck it all up! I hate your ass so much," she screamed, looking like a raving lunatic as she held the twelve-inch butcher knife high over her head in a threatening gesture.

"No! No, stop!" I screamed just as the tip of the shiny steel blade penetrated my heart and the first glimmer of blood appeared. I looked on in shock, unable to move.

Then I fell off the sofa, to the carpeted floor below, my piercing screams succeeding in jolting me fully awake. Sweat was pouring off me like I had stepped out of a sauna.

I pulled myself up, rested my back against the sofa, ecstatic to realize it was all a dream. I had fallen asleep and had had one of my crazy nightmares about Pilar. Damn, I couldn't get that chick out of my head. It was like she had a viselike grip on my brain and refused to let go. If anything, she had dug in deeper with her clawlike tendons. I didn't know what was wrong with me. Maybe Dre' was right. Maybe I did need to seek professional counseling. Maybe I couldn't handle it on my own.

What caused me the most frustration was that she was still out there, and I didn't know where. I hoped and prayed Pilar had moved on with her pathetic life, without me, but I didn't know for sure, and that scared me shitless. I knew it sounded absolutely crazy, but sometimes I could sense her. I'd turn and look behind me, but of course, she wouldn't be there.

No, I hadn't heard a peep from her since the e-mail she sent me over a year ago. However, I got the distinct impression that Pilar was very good at waiting. Plus, I had done my research, and I knew they, stalkers, could return and start the stalking all over again. The statistics were not in my favor.

It was late Saturday afternoon, and I had pretty much not done a damn thing most of the day. Sometimes, lately, all I wanted to do was sleep. Even in sleep, I wasn't always guaranteed peace. Pilar interrupted that, too, lately more and more often. Even out of my life, she was still stealing my joy.

I slowly walked into the kitchen and opened my stainless steel refrigerator, looked around at my choices, and retrieved the orange juice carton from the back. The bright orange carton was half full, and I made a mental note to pick up more. After pouring myself a cold glass and gulping it down in three swallows, I picked up my cell phone, which was lying on the countertop, on silent. A quick glance told me I had missed two calls and I had two messages, both from Bailey.

"Hey, sweetie. Check your e-mail. I forwarded you my flight itinerary. Can't wait to see you again."

I checked the second message.

"Call me later? Why do I always ask that question when I know you won't? Sometimes I can relate to Pilar from your movie, because it is hard loving someone when they won't or can't love you back. Well, I'm off for my jog."

"What the hell? What did love have to do with anything? Love shouldn't even be in the same sentence with my name and hers."

I had made up my mind that, after Bailey's next visit, I was going to cut off all contact with her. It was for her own good. She couldn't seem to comprehend what I had been telling her from the very beginning. And what was up with all that shit about identifying with Pilar? Had she lost her fucking mind? *Don't step to me with that drama.* That definitely wouldn't give her any brownie points in my book.

I know most would ask why I would wait until after her visit to cut all ties. I admit it. I'm a dog, still trying to become a reformed one. Bailey had some sweet pussy that I wanted to hit a few more times for old times' sake.

As for Dre', I couldn't wait to meet the woman who had him talking like a Hallmark greeting card. Little did I know, she was about to play God in both our lives.

"This is going to be your room," the aunt said excitedly, stepping aside so that the quiet and shy girl could enter and take a look around. "Don't be afraid. Come in, baby."

The girl slowly entered the pink and white bedroom and did a quick sweep of it with her lowered eyes. Her facial expressions didn't reveal if she liked it or not.

"I hope you like it. I wasn't sure if pink was one of your favorite colors," the aunt said, patiently waiting for an answer. "I think most girls love the color pink."

"Yes, ma'am," the girl said, never taking her eyes from the floor or wall or wherever, never making direct eye contact with the aunt.

"I know it's a little bare in here, but I figured you and I could go on a huge shopping spree and shop until we drop. You can pick out whatever you like to make this room all yours. We'll even get you one of those signs to hang on the door that states, 'Knock before you enter.'"

The aunt thought for just a second that she had glimpsed a small smile, almost unnoticeable. The entire time she had been trying to gain custody of her niece, she had never seen her smile. And what a beautiful smile she had.

The aunt walked over to the window and opened the curtains. "Let's get some sunshine up in here," she said, sitting on the edge of the full-sized bed. The aunt patted the bed beside where she sat. "Baby, come here and give me a hug. I am so happy to have you here. I love you so much. You do know that, don't you?"

The girl nodded her head.

"I know you have been through a lot over the years in your short life with my crazy-ass sister, but you are safe now. Okay?"

"Okay," the girl barely whispered.

"No one will hurt you again. I've never had any children of my own, and I always wanted a beautiful girl just like you."

There wasn't a response.

"Pilar? Please look at me," the aunt said with a warm smile.

The girl slowly looked up with big, innocent, but sad eyes, which were void of any light or joy. Her eyes revealed sadness and knowing beyond her years.

"Now that your mama is in jail and will be for a while, I pray she'll finally get some much-needed help, but I want you to know you can come to me for anything. I will never let anyone or anything hurt you ever again. I promise, and I'll take that to my grave." The aunt had spoken with the caseworker and had discovered the details of the file with a sense of horror and shame. Information was disclosed that had literally made her sick to her stomach. She'd barely made it to the restroom before losing her lunch. That was weeks ago.

"Okay," the girl said, with more conviction this time.

The aunt with the easy smile and loving heart pulled the girl to her for another big, comforting hug. Many more would follow during their time together. Her hugs would be like the treasure at the end of a rainbow.

For the first time in her life, the girl felt safe and protected. She would experience the feeling of love, unconditional love, and she would thrive. Her eyes would take on a bright light, and her soul would flour-

ish. However, a few years later, death's hand would steal it all away like a thief in the night. From that she would learn a valuable life lesson, that love is fleeting and you have to hold on to it as tight as you can, while you can.

Chapter 14

Pilar

I waited, watched, and listened patiently, double-checked my watch a few times. Patience was my middle name. This was the fun part, lying in wait for the prey to appear, not suspecting a thing. They were like calves being led to the slaughterhouse. Dressed in all black, from head to toe, with my hair pulled back in a tight ponytail, I strained to hear outside movement from inside the compact storage closet.

I had been waiting for close to an hour already. It didn't matter, because I had the patience of Job from the Bible. I knew it wouldn't be much longer, based on my observations from the earlier part of the week. Like I said, most people were creatures of habit. Bailey was no exception.

I had watched her comings and goings from my patio and had listened from the apartment next to hers—the one I had a three-month rental agreement on. I knew her little routine like the back of my hand. And just like I thought, she was a slut, plain and simple. Almost every other night, except for last night, a different man had his dick inside her. She claimed to love Xavier, based on the phone conversations I had listened in on, but just like in the Jay-Z song, she was just like a bus route, with everybody riding her.

Is that what Xavier really wanted or needed in his life? I could have been so good for him. I truly loved him. I loved him more than I loved myself, but somewhere deep inside, I realized it was too late for us. Some men would never be marriage material. Xavier would never change because he would always be controlled by the head in his pants. It was what it was.

Suddenly, I was pulled out of my reverie when I heard the sound of a door opening and closing. Then I heard the sound of movement, footsteps coming my way. That was my clue to ease the door of my hiding place, a hallway storage closet between our apartments, open a couple of inches wider and to adjust the black mask with eye, nose, and mouth openings over my head.

I cautiously peeked out. I had come too far to mess this up because of human error on my end. Yeah, that was the slut. Xavier couldn't seem to break away from the model-looking chick type if his life depended upon it. As I stared out at her, I was surprised at the intensity of my hatred. I was shocked that the severity of it didn't spill forth and overtake her on the spot. My disdain for her was so tangible, I expected her to turn and stare in my direction, fully aware of my presence. But she didn't. She took her time preparing for her daily run: applying lip gloss to her lips, securing her keys and water bottle.

I took her in from head to toe with utter disgust. She was tiny and perky and cute. Dressed in pink designer gear, she looked like a black Barbie. Xavier was too good for her. She didn't love him, just his deep pockets. For me, Xavier could be homeless, sleeping on a park bench, and I would still love him with everything I had inside. An image of Xavier flashed before my eyes, and I smiled. As Bailey adjusted her iPod, she looked my way. I quickly pulled back into the deep shadows, into the cover of darkness.

I had to admit Bailey had great taste. Her luxury apartment complex was very expensive, exclusive, and extraordinary. I had paid a pretty penny for a three-month rental agreement, but after my work was done, I would be long gone. Ghost. Yes, Bailey was a pretty little thing. I could understand why Xavier liked to fuck her repeatedly, but not for much longer. That was all about to change. And change was good, but I wasn't sure if Xavier would embrace it well.

I strained harder to hear, not moving, careful not to reveal my presence in the closet. I hated her with a blinding hatred at that moment in time. Xavier wanted her but not me. He screwed her but not me. She was everything I wasn't and would never be. I wasn't wholesome, without baggage, and undamaged, thanks to my mother, with her perverted appetites. The color red was now mixed with the raging hatred emitting from my very soul. Something inside my spirit erupted, and I became that other person. The one whose sole purpose was to survive by any means necessary. The one who could do very vicious things.

Just as she turned to skip down the stairs, Bailey stopped abruptly. She dropped down to tie the shoelace on her right foot, angled awkwardly against the stairwell. I saw images of Xavier performing oral sex on her, tasting her essence, sticking his beautiful black dick inside her and taking her to heaven. I hated her and everything she stood for!

Just as she stood up, I screamed out, "Bailey! You bitch!"

She turned in my direction, shock registered on her face, and I ran the short distance to her at full speed and delivered a single, forceful push. The expression

on her face as she stumbled down the stairs was priceless.

"Stay away from him! Do you hear me? Stay away
from him! There won't be another warning!"

I inched back, quickly stepping into the shadows.
I thought I heard a door open. I froze in my stance. I
quickly glanced over the railing to see her sprawled un-
naturally near the bottom of the flight of stairs, unmov-
ing but slightly moaning. And there was blood.

I smiled and quickly, like a thief in the night, entered
my unlocked apartment before the crowd came. They
always came after the fact. No one ever saved the innocent child when it was happening. There would be
questions. Did anyone hear anything? Did anyone see
anything out of the ordinary? By then I would be long
gone on my flight back to Houston and to Xavier and,
oh yeah, to Dre'.

I guessed Bailey wouldn't be going to Houston anytime soon. Mission accomplished. Next.

Chapter 15

Dre'

"Milan, you look breathtaking tonight," I stated, admiring her from across the dinner table and enjoying what I saw.

"Thank you, Dre'. You aren't looking too shabby yourself," she teased and smiled.

Damn, that smile did something to me—lit up my world and made me weak in the knees. "I'm glad you agreed to dinner, because I really wanted to see you again. To be honest, you have been on my mind since we met."

"How sweet, Dre', but I had already agreed to dinner before my trip."

"I know, but I thought you might be too tired to join me after you returned. Was your trip business related, or do you have family members in L.A.?"

She giggled in a girlish way. "Yeah, you could say it was business related."

"How was it?" I asked.

"It was very productive. I got a lot accomplished," she said as she took a sip of the glass of water with lemon directly in front of her. "A lot of obstacles came tumbling down. I believe I had a breakthrough."

"Good. Do you travel a lot?"

"For the past few months I have, but since my business is finished on the West Coast, I think I'll be around home more."

"Great. That will allow more time for me to get to know you better."

The waitstaff took that moment to approach with our entrées and drinks. We were silent as they arranged our plates and silverware in front of us and then left.

"This looks absolutely delicious," Milan stated, looking over her steaming seafood feast.

"Dig in. Enjoy."

"Wait. Go back, Dre'. You said I've been on your mind."

"You have. I couldn't even concentrate at work the other day. Kept thinking about the next time I would see you and that beautiful smile."

"Really? We just met. This is our first official date."

"I can't explain it, either. Like I was telling my best friend, you're a special lady, and I get a real good feeling from you."

"You've been talking about me to your friend?" she asked, dipping a jumbo shrimp into the red, tangy cocktail sauce.

"It's all good. He hasn't been too lucky in the relationship department lately, and I had to rub you in his face." I chuckled.

"That doesn't sound nice."

"No, it's not like that. Xavier and I go all the way back to childhood. We have always had this friendly rivalry between us. All in good fun."

"You two sound pretty close," she said, waiting for my response.

"We are. Close as blood brothers."

"Did you say his name is Xavier?"

"Yeah, Xavier Preston."

"Hmmm. That name sounds familiar."

"It should."

"Where have I heard that name before?"

"Right now he has the hottest number one movie in America. *Diary of a Stalker,*" I said, cutting into my juicy, well-done, mesquite-wood-grilled sirloin steak.

"Really? I haven't heard of it," Milan said, appearing not be interested.

I placed both hands on the table and stared at her, waiting for the laughter to start.

"What?" she asked. "Why are you looking at me like that?"

"Excuse me? You're kidding, aren't you?"

"Kidding about what?"

"You haven't heard of or seen *Diary of a Stalker* yet?"

She quietly chuckled. "No, I haven't. Should I?"

"I'm sorry. It's just that it's been the topic of conversation in homes and workplaces across the country."

"Well, I'm sorry, too. I don't go to the movies a lot, rarely watch TV, and with my hectic schedule, I simply don't have the time," she stated, taking a bite of her house salad.

"It's a date, then. You have to see the movie, because I am so proud of my man and I'm probably his number one promoter."

"You're a good friend. His triumphs are yours. That's nice."

"It's even more than that. The movie is based upon a real-life experience he had with a female stalker. The bitch, excuse my French, the chick turned his world upside down."

Suddenly I stopped talking because Milan had a look on her face that stopped me in mid-sentence. She looked ice cold. A chill ran down my spine.

"Is anything wrong? Did I say something to offend you?"

"No, go on. I'm listening," she said, with a bit of attitude lingering in her tone.

"I was saying that I'm simply happy that he was able to turn tragedy into triumph. He deserves this success. He really does. Xavier has worked extremely hard over the years, nothing was handed to him, and it finally paid off."

"Sounds like it has. You should be proud of your friend."

"I'm sure you'll have the opportunity to meet him soon."

"I would love to. I can hardly wait. Actually, I'm looking forward to it," she cooed.

The remainder of the night was uneventful but nice. Milan and I talked—well, mostly I talked—as we attempted to get to know each other a little better. There was a comfortable and unassuming quality she projected. I soon discovered that Milan had the unique ability to draw out personal information. I felt totally relaxed and at ease telling her about my early years, growing up in the mean streets of Houston. She took it all in, looked fascinated, hung on my every word. After a mouthwatering meal, we walked out of the restaurant hand in hand. I just knew I had found an exceptional lady, and I felt like the luckiest guy in the world.

Chapter 16

Xavier

Most people have heard the saying about how you can talk about a person and eventually talk them up. Well, I thought that was what I did with Kendall. I had been thinking so much about her lately that I thought her up.

I was shopping, something I absolutely hate, for a shirt in a department store at the Galleria mall and made a detour through the men's cologne department. When I glanced up from checking my cell phone messages, Kendall was standing less than fifty feet directly in front of me. I did a double take, because I thought I was seeing things. When I looked again, she was still there.

My heart literally skipped a few beats. At that moment, I realized I still had feelings for her. Deep inside, I had always known I still did. However, there was something about a man's ego that sometimes kept him from admitting certain truths to himself. Even though I was dead wrong to cheat on her, she still walked out on me. Kendall didn't try to work it out; instead, she chose to leave by breaking up. She literally threw the four-carat platinum engagement ring I'd bought her in my face after a few choice words, walked away, and never looked back. Today was my first time seeing her face-to-face since the breakup over two years ago.

Kendall turned and spotted me staring. For just a split second, a smile appeared on her beautiful face and her eyes revealed she was happy to see me. Just as quickly, her true feelings vanished as she pulled them back in. Her emotional shield went back up. Our eyes locked for a few seconds, until a distinguished-looking dude walked up and placed his hands around her tiny waist. She instantly looked away, averted her eyes, and giggled at something he whispered in her ear. She lovingly touched his cheek, and he leaned into her hand.

I turned away, because I felt like I was intruding on an intimate encounter. I was the odd man out. At that moment, I realized our time together had passed and nothing could ever be the same. Too much had been tarnished in the midst of my lies and betrayal.

When I turned around, Kendall was still standing there, looking at me expectantly. I walked over and closed the small distance between us. It felt like a mile separated us. As I closed the gap, I wasn't exactly sure how the mini reunion would play out.

"Hello, Kendall. How are you?" I managed to ask and kept a genuine-looking smile on my face at the same time.

To my surprise, she leaned in for a hug, wrapping her slim arms around my neck for a warm, brief embrace. All this while her husband—at least I assumed he was—looked on with a slight frown on his face.

"Hi, Xavier. It's good to see you. You look well."

"Same here," I said and truly meant it. Kendall did look beautiful; she was actually glowing.

In the midst of the hugs and sentiment, I almost forgot about her husband, until he cleared his throat several times.

"Baby, I would like for you to meet Xavier Preston," she stated, looking from him to me with a curious expression on her face.

I flinched when she called him baby. At one time, not too long ago, that name was reserved exclusively for me, sometimes whispered during the throes of passion, when I was buried deep inside her.

"Xavier, this is my husband, Dr. Vincent Linton."

"Good to meet you," I murmured as we shook hands halfheartedly.

"So, this is the famous author?" he asked like he had a bitter, vile taste on his tongue and couldn't get it off.

"That's what they tell me," I said, trying to inject humor into the situation.

"Xavier, I hear your movie is breaking all kinds of blockbuster records," Kendall remarked, attempting to break the obvious tension, which clung to the air like a thick, dense fog.

"You don't say?" he asked, sizing me up the entire time.

That pissed me off even more than standing there, pretending to be nice. I had to admit it—it was something that men did. I was guilty of sizing up another man myself. It was part of that king-of-the-jungle mentality; that my-dick-is-bigger-than-yours thing that was in play. I guessed it would be hard to meet the man who had almost married your wife and had sexed her on a regular basis.

"I could never quite figure out you creative types," he added.

"There's not much to figure out. We are just like everyone else," I retorted.

"I'm a surgeon," he stated, pushing his chest out farther. "I save lives on a daily basis. I literally have the power to give life or death. That makes sense to me."

"I agree, and I admire and respect your profession," I said, not breaking eye contact with him.

"Baby, shouldn't we be leaving?" Kendall interrupted. "You don't want to be late for your appointment," she said, gently pulling on his arm, attempting to lead him away and end this interrogation.

The doctor simply looked at her like she had lost her damn mind. He had every intention of playing out the purpose at hand—of making my profession out to be minuscule in relation to his. "What have I told you about butting into men's business?"

Kendall shrugged and backed down instantly.

"You have that movie out? *Diary*, uh?"

"*Diary of a Stalker*," I said slowly, like I was speaking to someone who was a little mentally challenged.

"Yeah, that's it. What's the point?"

"Excuse me? I don't understand your question."

"What value does that movie add to the quality of anyone's life? It's not like your little movie is a classic that will be viewed for generations to come, or critiqued and dissected by great literary minds."

I clenched and unclenched my jaw, thinking what a piece of work this guy was. He was unbelievable. I willed myself to remain quiet and let him talk so he could get all his resentment out.

"Did you enjoy displaying your relationship failures and infidelity to the world?" he asked, with an obvious smirk on his face.

"Movies and books are entertainment, Doctor. They make people laugh, cry, think, scream, and allow them simply to escape their day-to-day routine for a couple of hours. That's the value. They entertain."

"I don't need you to give me a lesson on the merits of movies. Actually, I am quite a movie buff. I simply don't partake of your kind of movie. I watch good movies, ones that have intrinsic value."

"To each his own," I said, trying to remain calm.

"Finally, something we can both agree on," he stated as he looked at me and sneered again.

"By the way, since you haven't seen it, you shouldn't assume it is a display of my relationship failures, as you say."

He looked to Kendall and nodded his head in her direction. "You lost her because you couldn't maintain a monogamous relationship. Real men lead with their brains and consider the consequences of their actions first."

"Baby, let's go," Kendall said, with anxiety steadily rising in her voice.

"Kendall told me every sordid detail. See, I love this woman with my heart and soul, and I would never lie down with dogs. I prove to Kendall how much I love her every day and night."

I noticed how he emphasized *night*. I was so angry at that moment that my head was throbbing. "I'm happy for the two of you. I wish you the best," I managed to spit out without an ounce of sincerity.

"Do you? Do you really?" he asked. "Writers make excellent liars. Is that a prerequisite?"

I didn't respond.

When his cell phone vibrated, he took his attention from me and quickly dismissed me. "Kendall, I need to take this call. Meet me near the exit, and don't be long."

When he walked off, after dismissing me like the help, I finally let my guard down and relaxed.

"Xavier, I'm really sorry about that," Kendal stated, looking embarrassed. "You aren't exactly one of his favorite people based on our history together."

"Is he always that high strung?"

"He doesn't usually act this way."

For some reason, I didn't believe her. "Unfortunately, I can understand, because I would be jealous, too, if I met the man who almost married my woman. But he won. He got you."

"Xavier, let's not go there," she stated, looking in the direction in which her husband had walked off.

"Are you happy?" I asked, looking at her intensely as I waited for her answer.

She hesitated. "I am. Very. He's a great provider."

"The last I heard—I may be wrong—but it takes much more than that to make a marriage work. Love is usually part of the equation."

"Silly, of course, I love him," she said with a nervous laugh.

"I've thought about you a lot lately, and I need to talk to you, Kendall."

"We are talking, and there's not much more to say," she stated, beginning to walk away.

"We can talk over lunch if you'd like. You choose. Our breakup, the way we parted, has bothered me, and I need to see that you are okay. I don't want you to hate me," I said, talking faster and following closely behind her.

"I am okay. I have a good life with a man that adores me."

"Just lunch, Kendall. We will be in a public setting. Food, maybe a couple of drinks, and two old friends talking, that's all," I said, throwing up my hands.

"No, I can't. I have to go," she stated, looking in the direction of her husband again.

"Here, take my business card. Call me. Please, Kendall," I replied, reaching into my wallet and handing one to her. Our fingers touched and briefly lingered as we made contact.

"Take care, Xavier," she said as she discreetly slipped my business card into her purse without once looking at it.

I watched her walk away.

If either of us had been paying attention, we would have noticed the mysterious, somewhat familiar female intensely watching us from a distance.

It was years later, and the young girl had grown into a beautiful young woman. Even though her mother would never admit it, the teenager's beauty now outshined hers, and if she searched even deeper within her soul, she would realize she was jealous of her daughter.

Mother and daughter coexisted as enemies under the same roof. There was an invisible line of unspoken hatred that separated them. The young girl's taste of unconditional love had ended with the death of her aunt. Now she felt like she was back in the den of evil.

"You think you're cute, don't you?" her mother asked, staring at her, with disgust clearly displayed on her face.

"No, Mama," the teenager said to her mother, who stood in the doorway of her tiny bedroom, watching as she completed her homework.

"Good. Because you ain't."

The teenager didn't respond. She had learned long ago to keep her answers simple and short, to keep her face frozen and devoid of any emotion. Most days she existed in a zombie-like state.

"Did you hear me? I regret the day I spread my legs for that no-good son of a bitch. Look at you. You got your ugly, disgusting looks from that bastard of a daddy of yours."

The teenager knew better than to inquire as to who or where this mysterious daddy was, and to be honest, after all this time had passed, she really didn't care. Men came with demands and pain.

"No man will ever want you. When they see you, they know what you are. No one could love such a lazy, stupid, ugly girl such as yourself."

The teenager tried to block it all out; she had heard these words, or worse, her entire life. She almost believed them . . . almost. Somewhere in the back of her rational mind, she knew there was someone out there waiting for her. And she knew someday she'd find him and her life would be happy and complete.

Chapter 17

Dre'

"Game shot," Xavier screamed as he extended his arm, expertly arched his right wrist, sent the basketball, which was suspended in air for a few seconds, and then hit nothing but net. "Booyah!" he exclaimed, doing a mini dance around the humid gym, causing a few people to look in our direction with amusement.

"Luck," I ventured, taking a seat on the third step up from the floor in the bleachers. I needed a few minutes to catch my breath; I wasn't working out like I should, and it was showing.

"Bullshit, man," Xavier said, taking a seat nearby and reaching for his black gym bag to retrieve bottled water. "That was known as skills. Serious skills, son. Something you wouldn't know if it bit you in the ass."

"You are making a lot of noise for a man who is up by only one game."

"Now, now, don't hate. I have to admit you gave me a run for my money. You almost had me, but everybody knows almost doesn't count," Xavier said.

Xavier took a big gulp of water and reclined against the back of the bleachers, looking at the people who milled around, wiping sweat from his face and neck.

I walked a couple of steps up, grabbed my bag, which contained water and a white towel. I proceeded to wipe sweat away and then quenched my thirst as well.

We were silent as we watched the action at the lower end of the court.

"Man, thanks again for coming out to speak with the teams today," I said.

"Not a problem. It was my pleasure. You know I love doing events like this, especially in this neighborhood. This is where you and I grew up. This place made us the men we are today."

"Do you ever think about all the ones we lost along the way?"

"Some didn't even live to see twenty-one, others are in prison, and some just let the streets beat them down, and now they are strung out on drugs or worse."

"Poverty and lack of hope are the two bitches of the hood."

"There are those like us who made the decision to get out, do better, become something, and give back," Xavier said.

"Those are the ones I want to reach. The ones who realize there is a better life outside this neighborhood."

"And you will. One kid at a time."

Xavier had spent most of the morning talking with various boys' basketball teams, with boys between the ages of nine and eighteen. Now, most had left for a huge tournament on the other side of town. I volunteered at least once a month at the recreation center that we used to hang out at as young boys, back in the day. Back then, this was my home away from home. Now this was my way of giving back, along with generous donations. Xavier and I had finished up a few one-on-one games. We were tied until that last game shifted the score in Xavier's favor.

"Man, the way they were holding on to your every word, you would've thought we had a major league player up in this joint." I laughed and took another swig of water and pressed the plastic bottle against my forehead.

"Don't hate," Xavier said, finishing up the last drops of his bottled water.

"I'm not. Man, you had me all amped up and excited, had me wanting to be a damn writer."

"Man, you stupid. Stupid, I tell you."

"No, seriously, I believe these kids can only aspire to what they see. Unfortunately, you know as well as I do that most of them see drug dealers, pimps, hustlers, and wannabe rappers as their idols on a daily basis. That's what they know. I figure if I can bring in people from different professions, they can see that they can become and be anything they want to. After all, we have a black man in the White House."

"Speak it."

"I think a few of the boys are interested in starting an investment firm," I said with a real sense of pride in my voice.

"For real?"

"I'm serious. You know I talk to them all the time about finances and how it's never too early to start investing money and obtaining wealth. Who knows? Maybe you were talking to future stockbrokers or even writers."

"That's cool. I'm proud of the difference you are making in these boys' lives, and I am seriously thinking about joining One Hundred Black Men of America with you," Xavier said.

"Me too, man. I can't explain the feeling I feel when I know I've reached one of them. You can almost see the lightbulb go off in their heads. One Hundred Black Men is a great organization that gives back to the community with solid results."

"Back in the day, who would have thought we'd be here—instilling some knowledge and wisdom?"

We laughed.

"Of course, there are the knuckleheads who won't listen. You know, the wannabe thugs and gangbangers. Not a word you said reached them, and it doesn't matter how much I talk with them. Some are simply made out of a bad cloth. They don't get it and never will," I said.

"Yeah, and they'll wind up in prison or dead by age twenty-one. A lost generation of young men is what we are seeing today, and that's a damn shame."

"But mostly, these are good kids growing up in difficult surroundings and circumstances. They can't control where they are born or what they are born into, but we know it doesn't matter where you're from but where you're going."

"I feel you, because there but for the grace of God go us," Xavier said.

"You ready for another round?" I asked.

"You ready to get that ass spanked again?"

"Who's going to do it?" I asked, standing up.

"Please, earlier I was just warming up. You ain't seen nothing yet." Xavier walked over, picked up the nearest basketball, and started shooting. Some shots he made; others bounced off the wall or the rim of the basketball net. "Dre', you will never guess who I ran into yesterday."

"Who?" I asked, grabbing the ball and shooting a few times.

"Guess."

"Man, I don't know. Pilar?"

"Oh, you got jokes today."

"What? You didn't want to see Pilar? Afraid she would kidnap you and carve her name on your chest with a blade?"

"Man, that shit is not funny."

"I'm not laughing. You were the one chained to a hotel bed while she whipped your ass with a mini whip. That's not cool. That's demented."

I looked at Xavier and tried to maintain a straight face. He stared back, silently daring me to start laughing.

"I arrived at your hotel to rescue your ass, thinking I'm going to have to fight myself out of a bad situation, and there you are, wrapped up in a sheet, looking like black Jesus. And then I see the whelp marks where old girl fucked you up like Kunta Kinte. No, that shit is not funny." I then proceeded to laugh so hard, my stomach hurt.

"Fuck you, man," Xavier said.

When I finally recovered, I said, "Xavier, I can laugh at it now because you survived. You survived stronger and wiser."

"Very true."

We pumped fists, then continued to take turns shooting back and forth.

"I ran into Kendall and her new husband."

That made me pause. "I bet that shit was awkward as hell. Damn, it couldn't have been me."

"Tell me about it," Xavier said.

"So what's up? What did she say? Better question, what did *you* say?"

"Once I recovered from the shock of seeing her standing there, looking beautiful, I wasn't sure what to say."

I laughed. "Mr. Writer was at a loss for words. That's a first."

"I thought she was a figment of my imagination. Man, she took my breath away, and when she leaned in to hug me, I almost forgot old dude was standing there."

"Hugs? I'm surprised she didn't slap the spit out of your mouth."

"To be honest, me, too. I still feel guilty over how our relationship ended, and I still think of her at times."

"I bet you do. A man always wants what he can't have, and now that another man is stroking that, well, I'm sure it is killing you to think about what you could have had."

"I don't need you to attempt to read my feelings like some amateur psychologist."

"Call it what you must, but you know it was killing you to see her with mister," I said as I threw the ball at him.

"Dude was staring me down, giving me the once-over."

"Damn."

"Tried to downplay my profession and give me the virtues of a surgeon."

"Damn," I said, biting my balled-up fist. "Ouch."

"Yeah, he was an arrogant son of a bitch. He definitely seemed like the controlling type who would have Kendall on lockdown."

"Maybe, but that's not your concern anymore."

"I realize that, but you don't know how badly I wanted to kick his pompous ass."

"Man, who are you talking to? The public gets to see the articulate, poised, well-spoken author. I know the side that can get downright grimy and dirty."

"Damn straight."

"How did this little meeting end?"

"I kept my cool and tried to persuade Kendall to meet me for lunch."

"In front of her husband?"

"No, fool. He had walked off by then to answer a phone call."

"What's the point of lunch? It's a done deal, man. Just learn to lie in the bed you made."

"Like I said, I feel guilty. It's almost like I need to apologize and right my wrongs from the past before I can move forward."

"I feel you. However, I honestly don't know if you'll ever get that opportunity with Kendall. I always warned you about fucking around on that sweet thing."

"You did, but my other head spoke louder while Pilar was whispering in my ear."

"My advice is to leave that happily married woman alone and move on with your life. That's real talk. Anything other than that is asking for trouble."

"Too late. Kendall looked me up on Facebook, e-mailed my in-box, and we are meeting for lunch next week."

"Damn! Playa, playa!"

"No, it's not even like that. I just want to make sure she's happy, apologize, and leave on a cordial note."

"Sure, you keep telling yourself that, because I know the deal. I know you. Don't get bit in the ass again, Xavier."

Chapter 18

Pilar

Afterward, after sexing with Michael, I always felt safe and sound, in a real good place. That was how I felt now, in a good, safe place. That was something I had always placed a huge premium on as an adult. No one could hurt or punish me, or make me do vile, disgusting acts that I didn't want to. Those days were long gone—forever.

Mama was dead, hopefully rotting in hell for all eternity, but sometimes I heard her in my head, and lately, it was more and more. She came when I wanted to sleep or when I was focusing on a task at hand. Mama always came with the same relentless chatter. It consumed my head to capacity, and I would feel as if it would burst.

That man doesn't want you except for one thing. He doesn't love you. How could he? Look at yourself. Have you looked in a mirror lately? Why don't you do something to that damn hair?

You are one ugly creature. No one would ever guess I gave birth to you. How many pounds have you gained?

I know I taught you better. You always get paid. Nothing in life is free. Your pussy is as good as an American Express black card. How could you let him climb on top of you and stick his dick inside you without him showing you the money? You are disgusting.

All that sweating and moaning and groaning. You sounded like barnyard animals.

You are damaged goods, girl. Don't any normal, decent man want you.

She would do that high-pitched cackle I always hated. I would place my hands over my ears in an attempt to block out her insistent chatter, or hit my forehead over and over with my fist until she shut the hell up.

"Wow, that was good," Michael stated, already beginning to slip into a semi-after-sex mode.

I smiled and snuggled closer, resting my head on his chest. Michael was light skinned, athletically built, intelligent, just the type of man women wanted to be with.

"You are always so intense when we have sex," he said, smoothing down my hair and sighing. "That's what I love about you."

"Do you?"

"Yes. That and how mysterious you are."

"I'm not mysterious, Michael," I stated, relaxing to his touch. If I were a cat, I would have purred.

"Yes, you are, Pilar. Hell, you know everything there is to know about me, and I know very little about you except for the basics."

"You know the most important things," I said, reaching for his semi-erect dick.

"That I do." He laughed, rolling back on top of me and pinning my hands above my head.

Bitch, you need to have him pay you if you are going to constantly let him go up inside you, Mama screamed. *He's a greedy little bastard.*

I frantically shook my head to clear my thoughts.

"What's wrong, baby? Michael asked, spreading my legs farther apart with his knees. "Are you still having those headaches you mentioned?"

"No, I'm fine. I'm just thinking about how good we are together. Don't you think?"

He grunted as he slowly entered me again. He slid in easily and expertly; I had lost count of how many times we had gone at it.

"Michael? Did you hear me?" I asked.

"Hmmm. Yeah, baby. Whatever you say. Damn, you have some good stuff," he grunted.

"Do you think they suspect anything at work?"

"Like what?"

"That we are seeing each other?"

By now, he was slowly thrusting in and out of me, with his large hands wrapped around my neck.

"Shhh. Move with me."

"Answer my question," I demanded.

"No, we are discreet. They don't know I'm banging you every chance I get." He laughed.

I frowned. "I hope I'm more than that to you. I don't want to be your jump-off."

"Baby, shhh. You're going to make me lose this nut that's coming."

I looked up at him and tried my best to get out from underneath him. Michael, in turn, struggled to prevent my escape. Nothing was going to stop him from nutting.

"Shit, Pilar. Stop acting so crazy all the damn time. Of course I care for you, or I wouldn't spend so much time with you. You even have a key to my home, and I don't randomly give those out."

"You care for me, but do you love me?"

"Baby, right now all I can offer is that I care for you."

I pondered his response for a few seconds. "Do you think you could love me down the line?"

Michael pinched the tip of my nose and appeared to be deep in thought. "I think so. You are so damn adorable, except for when you are asking too many damn questions."

I smiled.

He smiled. "Now, where were we? Oh yeah, I was getting lost in your good loving," he stated, nuzzling into my neck and sending quivers up and down my arms.

"Are you seeing Linda, the entertainment reporter from work?" I asked out of the clear blue.

He froze for a brief second. No one else would have caught it, but I did.

"Well, are you?"

"Why on earth would you ask me that?"

"I've heard rumors." I didn't mention that I had seen her with my own eyes entering his home on more than one occasion.

"Well, there you go. Since when do you listen to office rumors? Writers love to fabricate the smallest truth."

"I hope you aren't lying, Michael, because I couldn't handle a lie. I have to be your one and only. That's the only way we can be together. If I'm not, then . . ."

With that, Michael bit down on my exposed right nipple. "I hear you loud and clear. You have nothing to worry your pretty little head about. Now, can we please finish what we started before you give me blue balls?"

"Sure, on one condition," I said seriously, with a straight face.

"What's that?" he asked curiously.

"I want you to fuck me hard, because I need to feel every inch of you."

"I think I can handle that request."

Michael did just that; he gave all of himself. He made me feel every delicious inch; I couldn't tell where he began and I left off, because he was so deep inside.

Michael wrapped his hands around my neck again and squeezed, lightly at first. Then he applied more pressure. Just as my oxygen level was being cut off, I felt a tremendous orgasm coming on. Michael sensed it, too, because his eyes rolled back in his head and I could tell he was gone—to another level of ecstasy.

He squeezed again, and I came. I came so hard, it scared me. Rivers flowed. Lightning flashed. Right before I joined Michael and saw ecstasy, I whispered, "I love you, Xavier."

Michael was so far gone that he didn't hear me or perhaps didn't even care.

Chapter 19

Xavier

Life had a funny way of throwing unexpected twists and turns your way and watching the pieces fall where they may.

I definitely wasn't expecting to receive a Facebook e-mail from Kendall. Yes, at the advice of my publicist, I had created a page. However, when she suggested we meet for lunch at one of my favorite restaurants, which used to be *our* favorite restaurant, I certainly wasn't going to analyze it. Like always, I didn't think it through, simply reacted to the opportunity that presented itself.

As I found myself pulling into the restaurant parking lot, I was slightly distracted. I had received a somewhat disturbing phone call that Bailey had been involved in a terrible accident and was in the hospital. I still had not received the full story, only that she had somehow tumbled down the stairs in her apartment building and had suffered a concussion, broken arms, and a broken leg. All that information I received from her agent.

To be honest, I was kind of looking forward to seeing her this week. She was scheduled to arrive on Thursday evening; however, I guessed that wasn't happening now or anytime soon.

Apparently, Bailey was very lucky, because she could have broken her neck during the fall. On the other end, she had a long recovery ahead of her. I had my newly hired assistant send flowers and a card, and asked her agent to keep me abreast of her condition and to let me know if there was anything I could do. When Bailey was physically able and feeling better, I hoped to speak with her.

All thoughts of Bailey were quickly pushed to the back of my mind when I walked into the trendy spot and spotted Kendall waving me over near the bar area.

I closed the short distance between us. "Hi, Kendall," I stated, hugging and kissing her on the cheek. "You look nice."

"Hello, and thank you," she said, leaning into the hug a bit too long as her breasts rubbed against my chest.

"Have you been waiting long?"

"No, just a few minutes."

"Good, because I was running a little late and the traffic didn't give me any breaks, but here I am."

"Let me get the hostess, and we can be seated. I was just waiting up here for you," she said, waving the friendly hostess over.

"Sounds good."

A few minutes later we were seated in a semiprivate, cozy, very intimate section of the restaurant. I took the liberty of pulling out her chair and casually walked around to seat myself. I stared at Kendall, waiting for her to speak first, as she took a sip of water.

"What?" she asked, noticing that my attention was focused on her. "You are staring at me."

"Nothing. I just can't believe you contacted me on Facebook, and, well, here we are, together. I didn't think I would ever see the day when we could be civil to one another, or should I say, you to me?"

"Don't feel so shocked, Xavier. People grow and mature with time. Besides, you did say you wanted to speak with me, and to be honest, I was curious as to what you could possibly have to say."

"Yeah, but you were so adamant about not seeing me," I said, watching her intently.

"Well, I had a chance to think about it and . . ." Her voice trailed off.

"And what? Go on."

"After the scene that played out at your house, we never really had closure. I had my say, stormed out with a broken heart, and that was pretty much it. End of story."

"True," I stated, still unable to stop myself from staring at the woman I used to love. "You were pretty upset that day."

"That's an understatement," she said with nervous laughter.

There was always that one woman you never forgot no matter how hard you tried. Kendall was it for me. Believe me when I say I had tried. The others, and there were many, didn't mean anything to me, nada. They were simply distractions and then on to the next one. The others were something to do, someone to do, something to pass the time while in the different cities of my book tours, random, meaningless faces and bodies. Kendall, she was the real deal, and I blew it by sleeping with Pilar, a crazed stalker.

"How have you been?" she asked, looking everywhere but in my eyes and at my face. I knew she was asking only out of politeness, to keep the conversation flowing.

"Kendall, you don't have to be nervous around me. We used to be comfortable with one another," I stated, instinctively reaching for her small hand.

She reacted by slowly pulling it away and placing it in her lap. "That was then, and this is now. Things change. Much has changed. I've changed."

"That they do, sometimes because of the stupidity of others. I want to take this time to apologize for any hurt I may have caused. I didn't mean to hurt you. Believe me when I say that was the farthest thing from my mind."

"But you did hurt me." Her eyes finally found mine and settled within, giving me a glimpse of the pain and betrayal she'd suffered because of my actions.

"I know I did, and if I could, I would take it all back. I would rewind time. I can only hope that you will accept my apology someday. Kendall, I was such a fool, but I never stopped loving you, and I do realize what a good woman I lost because of my infidelity."

Our waiter chose that exact moment to step to us for drink and lunch orders. I think Kendall was relieved that the conversation had been briefly interrupted, because of my declaration of still loving her. I had surprised even myself with that statement.

Kendall and I placed our orders, and it was weird because it was what we had always ordered in the past, whenever we dined there. That much hadn't changed. As the waiter hurried away and stopped at a table nearby, Kendall was quiet. She looked around, played with her hair, which she now wore in a stylish cut and basically did everything but address what I had stated.

"Do you, Kendall?"

"Do I what?"

"Forgive me."

She paused for only a second. "I did that a long time ago so I could move on with my life. I was so consumed with hating you and what you did to me, to us, that I became stagnant. I had to forgive you in order to save myself."

"Thank you."

"There is no need to thank me. Understand I did it for myself, not for you. Be very mindful of the fact that I didn't forget. I know what type of person you are, Xavier, and you will probably always be that way. I knew that going in. Stupid me. I really thought my love, our love, was greater than what you put me through."

I lowered my head in shame because I didn't know how to respond. Now I was the one unable to meet her lingering, accusing eyes.

"Watching *Diary of a Stalker* shed some light on the situation you were dealing with, and my heart unfroze a bit more. If it hadn't been for my husband, I don't know if I would have survived our breakup. I loved you so much, Xavier, but I couldn't live a life filled with lies and infidelity. So, I loved myself more and moved on."

I finally looked up. "Do you love him?"

She smiled, a haunting smile filled with mystery. "Yes. I do love him. Not in the way I loved you. That was different. Our love, what you and I shared, was intoxicating, breathless, and passionate. I love my husband in a less complicated way than what we shared."

I was silent, speculating on the meaning behind her words, reading between the lines.

"Did you expect me to say no?" Kendall asked.

I didn't respond. To be honest, I wasn't quite sure what I expected her to say.

"I'm happy, Xavier, happier than I have been in a long time. You hurt me. I couldn't eat. I couldn't sleep. My studies suffered, and I went into a deep depression. With the support of my family and church, I survived."

"I'm sorry, Kendall."

"I never wanted to be one of those women."

"What kind of woman is that?"

"The type of woman who lets a man break her down to the core and then hates all men because of one bad apple."

"Ouch. I guess I deserved that. I didn't mean—"

"Hear me out. Do I miss you and wonder what we could have become together? Yes, all the time, but I realize life is a cycle of mishaps, adventures, traveled paths, and then sometimes the fork in the road throws a detour. Two people can come together but not really complement each other. Our time has passed, so I'm asking you to please let me go."

"Kendall, you know I wish you nothing but the best. My one regret is that things didn't work out between us. Believe it or not, I want you to be happy, even if it is with someone besides myself. I wish you the very best that life has to offer."

"That is sweet," she said, giving me a look of adoration that I hadn't seen since before our breakup.

"I mean it. It's straight from the heart. So, are we cool?"

"We're cool, Xavier."

For the first time since we sat down to dine, Kendall appeared relaxed.

"Tell me what's going on in your life, Mr. Writer-Slash-Executive-Producer. I am so proud of your success. I remember when we would lie in bed and talk about our dreams and goals for the future. Remember that?" She smiled, thinking about the good times we shared.

"Of course. You were going to finish law school, pass the bar the first time around, and become this big-shot attorney. How could I forget all the happy times we spent together? There were definitely more happy than bad, and I'll always cherish those memories."

"Yeah, I remember how you would always hog the sheets, too."

We laughed, and another layer slipped away.

"To answer your question, I'm chillin' for a minute."

"Oh, you chillin', huh?" She laughed, mocking me. "Sure you are."

"What is that supposed to mean?" I questioned.

"Xavier, you don't know how to relax. You don't know the meaning of the word. That's what I used to like about you. . . . You were always so driven."

"Seriously, I'm trying to enjoy my success and get my life in order. I'm not getting any younger. I'm attempting to get my priorities straight and be the great man I know I can be."

"You'll get there. We are all a work in progress," Kendall shared.

"Thank you. That means a lot coming from you."

She smiled.

I smiled back.

"You aren't working on anything?"

I paused, playfully looked up at the ceiling, pretending I hadn't heard her question.

"Xavier?"

"Huh? Did you say something?"

"See, I knew it! It's in your blood. You have to write and follow your passion, or you aren't complete."

"That's what I always loved about you, Kendall. You always got me. Got me like no other." My eyes softly caressed her, and she blushed.

She looked down at her hands, unwilling to read the unspoken words my eyes were sending.

"Kendall, am I making you uncomfortable? I don't mean to. I'm simply being honest. I have decided to try honesty going forward."

"I'm okay. It's just hard knowing what we could have had together. By now, we would have been married, probably working on starting a family," she explained, looking melancholy. "Remember, we were going to have a girl and boy and name them . . ."

"Alexandria and Alexander," I said, completing her sentence for her.

She caught my eye and smiled a bittersweet smile. "You remembered."

I cleared my throat. "Of course. What's going on in your life, Mrs. Married Lady?" I asked to change the subject.

She smiled a big toothy smile. "I passed the bar exam the first time," she said, pretending to pop her collar.

"Congratulations, baby! I'm so proud of you."

She blushed. "Don't call me that."

"What?"

"Baby."

"I'm sorry. Habit, I guess. Should I attach *esquire* to your name now?"

"You are silly."

"You always liked it."

I instinctively reached for her hand, and this time she didn't pull away.

"I am so proud of you. I know this was your dream, and I'm certain you are going to make a wonderful attorney."

"Thank you. I appreciate that, Xavier."

For a few seconds we were lost in each other's eyes. Our silence spoke volumes.

"Does he know you're here?" I asked to break the spell and bring us back to reality.

"What do you think?"

"I don't know. That's why I asked."

"Of course not."

"Why did you risk coming here today?"

"One word. *Closure.* I needed to hear what you had to say so that I could have some form of closure. I have moved on, but I needed to face you one last time."

"Do you feel that's what we accomplished today?"

"I do."

"I feel we opened up a whole new can of worms. I want you so bad right now, Kendall. I miss you, and I realize what a wonderful woman I lost due to my infidelity, foolishness, and weakness."

She blushed and looked around hastily to make sure no one had heard me. "Xavier, you can't say things like that. It's over for us," she explained, like she was talking to a child. "I'm a married woman."

"I can't help it. I'm simply being honest."

She shook her head and closed her eyes.

"Don't you feel anything sitting across from me? Aren't any of the old feelings resurfacing, or did they ever really leave?"

"Please. Don't do this."

"Just answer my question. If you say no, I won't believe you. It shows in your body language, and I could always read your body."

Kendall never had the opportunity to respond to my question because a loud crash behind us altered the course of the conversation and our waiter chose that moment to bring our drinks and meals over.

Most of the remainder of lunch was spent drinking, eating, talking of trivial matters, catching up, and avoiding our obvious attraction, which was like a tangible presence of its own that pulsated to its own beat.

A New Beginning

The dark, hooded figure stood in the wispy shadows, unseen from the secluded street, and patiently waited. The roaring fire blazed far and wide, sizzling, popping, and hissing. She thought it was beautiful the way the brilliant flames literally danced back and forth in the stillness, disrupting the silence and demanding attention. The air was alive as it crackled, sparked, and pulsed with electricity and energy.

The flames hypnotized her and released within a sense of power that she never knew she possessed. The higher the flames grew and the louder the fire roared, the more powerful, unstoppable, and confident she became. This feeling was new to her, liberating, exhilarating down to her core.

It was almost as if an unseen transformation was taking place as she lurked in the shadows. She was shedding an old identity and claiming a new and improved one. Under the cover of darkness, a rebirth was happening, with no one to witness it but the twinkling stars and cloudless sky above.

By the time the fire department arrived, it would be too late for her mother and the man she called Daddy-the stepfather whose bed she also shared, sometimes along with her mother. Yes, it would be much too late for them. She prayed the fiery gates of hell had already opened and welcomed them in as one of their *own. She reveled in the fact that they would live in eternal damnation. She thought that was a suitable sentence.*

Chapter 20

Pilar

I could barely contain myself as I hastily made my way to the front door of the restaurant. The exit sign was a welcome sight. I wanted to hit something, hurt somebody so badly that I was shaking uncontrollably with furor.

That stupid bitch, I silently screamed in my head. "*Stupid.* How dare she?" I muttered to myself as I bumped into a startled waiter as I made my quick departure out the heavy double doors of the exit. "Slut. A married woman and still shamefully throwing herself at Xavier."

I had taken a quick right and had heard dishes crash to the floor, causing heads to turn toward the source of the noise. I hadn't uttered an apology or even paused for a second. I was on a mission. I had to get out of there before I exploded with a vengeance.

"I'll show her ass, again. Hardheaded . . . simply hardheaded."

I knew Xavier was a male whore, but I thought Miss My-Shit-Don't-Stink was decent. She absolutely was not going to have her cake and eat it, too. Not on my watch. If I couldn't have him, why should she? She had a man, and I had no one, and probably never would. It just wasn't fair. My life hadn't been fair since I came out of my mother's womb.

I calmed down slightly as fresh air greeted me. Restaurant patrons seated near the front were still curiously looking out the window, confused over my frantic departure. I forced myself to calm down as I made my way to my car and pressed UNLOCK on my keypad. I somehow managed to place myself in the driver's seat. *Breathe. Breathe. Take deep calming breaths. Think happy thoughts.* Yeah, I was going to fix her ass and good. I'd show her. When was she going to learn once and for all that Xavier was no longer her man?

They were always hardheaded. They would learn the lesson for a short time and then backpedal. I knew it was hard to get over Xavier; I, of all people, realized that. There was something about him that drew a woman in and took over her life, devoured her alive and dominated her thoughts. As much as I hated him, I loved him even more. There truly was a thin line between love and hate. And I was about to show Xavier the true meaning of hate. When I was finished, he would have a PhD in the subject.

I managed to drive myself back to my tiny apartment on the other side of town. During the process, I managed not to hurt myself or an innocent driver or pedestrian. I was so mad. Correction, I was beyond mad. I was pissed! I never stayed mad for long because I knew how to get even.

Women like Kendall always thought they were privileged and delicate and special. Even from my corner view in the back of the restaurant, I saw how Xavier looked at Kendall. He never, not even once, looked at me like that. He still loved her. He still adored her. No doubt about it—he would take her back in a New York minute. Not! Not if I had anything to do with it.

I smiled because a plan was already being formulated in my mind as I unlocked my front door and entered my world.

Chapter 21

Dre'

"Sure. That sounds like a plan to me," I said with a huge smile on my face.

"I'll see you tomorrow," she whispered in a singsong tone, and I imagined her looking all sweet and sexy in a stunning see-through teddy that left nothing to my imagination.

"Can't wait," I said, hanging up my landline.

I still hadn't quite figured out what Milan had done to me. Ever since our dinner date, I couldn't seem to get her off my mind. Anyone who knew me definitely realized this was uncharacteristic. Dre' Walker didn't fall head over heels in love or entertain sappy romantic notions. I had stopped believing in fantasies a long time ago.

Sure, at thirty-eight, almost thirty-nine, I had been married and divorced two times. I knew the real deal when it came to women, love, and relationships. Hell, I could pen a relationship-based book like Steve Harvey! For years now I had been telling Xavier he should ghostwrite one for me.

Relationships were not all they were cracked up to be. Women changed on you as often as you changed your socks. In the beginning, they could be as sweet as honey. They stroked my ego and listened while I talked, like I held the secret to life in my words. They would give good loving on a regular basis. They kept their hair looking good, dressed sexy but classy, and made sure they smelled good. Sure, each one seemed like the ideal, perfect woman, but I had lived long enough to know the perfect woman didn't exist.

I hadn't quite figured it out, but there was something about placing a diamond ring on a woman's finger—the larger the carat, the better—and promising to love and cherish a woman forever that changed the nature of a relationship for the worse. My forever never lasted longer than three years, because shortly after the wedding I never knew who I had up in my house or bed. Everything changed. I could always count on that. Okay, I admit the first year was always fine, the honeymoon stage, but after that things always went downhill in a quick hurry, like an unstoppable avalanche.

I wouldn't say that each and every time it was my ex who was to blame—I played my part. I realized without a doubt that I was not Mr. Perfect, either, but when I was faithful to you, elevating your lifestyle, making you come in the bedroom, and you still couldn't respect me, keep my house clean, and cook my meals . . . Well, then we had a problem. I knew I was a traditional man when it came to relationships.

Xavier was always saying I scared my wives away with my Neanderthal ways and ideas. I wanted my woman to be a woman, and not someone trying to wear my pants. As for Milan, I had a really good feeling about her. I could barely wait for our date tomorrow night.

Chapter 22

Xavier

"Khai, don't forget to send flowers and a get-well card to Bailey out in California," I said, speaking into my cell phone.

"Already done, Mr. Preston."

"What did I tell you? Please call me, Xavier."

"Oh, okay, Mr. . . I mean, Xavier," Khai stated.

"That's more like it," I said, walking upstairs from my morning workout and wiping sweat from my face with the white towel draped around my neck.

"Xavier, again, thank you so much for this opportunity. I can't believe I'm the assistant to the one and only Xavier Preston. Students in my creative writing program would die to be in my shoes."

"You deserve it, Khai. You were definitely the best out of all the candidates interviewed. Besides, you have done a spectacular job in just the few weeks you've worked for me."

"Thank you."

"By the way, you are more than welcome to work from my home office anytime you like, whether I'm here or not. You have the spare key and security codes."

"If it's okay with you, I would rather not. I prefer to work from your office only when you are there." I detected a slight hesitation in her voice.

"That's fine, Khai. Whatever works for you. I have no problem with that as long as the projects get completed."

"I appreciate that."

"May I ask why you prefer not to be in my home alone?"

"Well," she began. "I always . . ." She hesitated.

"It's okay," I said reassuringly.

"I always feel like I'm being watched when I'm there alone. You know how the tiny hairs can stand up on the back of your neck and arms?"

"Yes."

"Well, that happens to me. Plus, I sometimes hear strange sounds, and one day I'm pretty sure I heard voices and something crash to the floor upstairs."

As I stopped in mid-step on the staircase, I didn't say anything for a few seconds.

"I know I sound totally insane, but . . ."

"I'm sure it's your overactive imagination," I kidded. "I have top-of-the-line security, so you have nothing to worry about, Khai. You're safe here. Maybe you shouldn't have seen my movie."

"Actually, I saw it twice. It was just that good."

We laughed, and just like that the subject was changed.

"That's all for now, Khai. I'm going to take a quick shower and grab lunch."

"Okay, Mr. Preston, I mean, Xavier. I'll get on those assignments you gave me earlier right away."

As I pushed END on my cell phone, I thought back to Khai's words. Sometimes I felt like I was being watched, as well, but I had totally chalked it up to what had happened between Pilar and me in the past. I still sometimes looked behind me when I was walking outside. I shook my head to clear my thoughts as I walked upstairs to my bedroom. I was well aware of the chill bumps that had suddenly broken out and rushed up and down my arms like an army of angry ants.

Now a beautiful young woman, she recalled the first time she met Dr. Leeda Smith. She didn't know what to make of her. She remembered sizing her up when she thought Dr. Smith wasn't looking. Dr. Smith was very pretty in a refined way, and she smelled good. The young woman didn't particularly trust women and kept them at a distance. She found women to be jealous, conniving, and deceiving. However, she found herself fascinated by Dr. Smith. She particularly liked the way Dr. Smith spoke and pronounced each word articulately and precisely. Dr. Smith wore her trademark glasses perched on the very tip of her nose, but they never fell off. For some reason, she decided she could trust her. In the years to come, they would form a strong, unbreakable bond.

This was her third visit, and she was in her usual seat on the sofa, near the very edge, as far away from the doctor as possible. She nervously tapped her fingers on the leather armrest.

"How was your week?" Dr. Smith asked, appearing genuinely interested.

"Okay, I guess. Nothing special."

"Just okay? By the way, you look pretty today. Those colors look great on you."

"Thank you," the woman replied shyly. She was not used to receiving compliments, at least not from a female. The only other female who had ever been kind to her was an aunt who passed away suddenly. There were a few female teachers, too, now that she thought about it. Some showered her with genuine acts of kindness.

"What do you feel like talking about today?"

The young woman shrugged her shoulders, looking down at the floor, continuing to tap her fingers in a rhythmic manner.

"If you can't decide, that's fine. I'll decide for us this time."

The young woman remained silent. She still hadn't opened up yet.

"Is your hot tea okay?"

"It's fine," she said, carefully lifting up the decorative saucer and cup from the coffee table.

"Good. I drink at least a cup a day, and it always calms and relaxes me."

Dr. Smith moved to sit across from her and smiled. The young woman enjoyed how comfortable she made her feel.

"Let's start out talking about your mother, because she played a pivotal role in your life, no matter how destructive it may have been. Are you still having nightmares about her?"

"Yes."

"Don't worry, sweetie. I promise you, I am going to make that scary monster go away."

The young woman smiled for the first time that day.

Chapter 23

Pilar

It had been a few days since the restaurant debacle. I was still angry. My anger, seeping deep inside my soul, was like a scab that never healed because I kept picking at it within my mind. I almost, just almost, picked up the phone and dialed my friend/psychiatrist, Leeda. In fact, I had actually dialed the first few digits when I realized I could handle this in my own way—with my own street justice. I could serve it up with the best.

Kendall was no match for me; dealing with her was mere child's play. I still had to wait a couple of days before my plan could be fully carried out. After that, I was fairly certain she would not come anywhere near Xavier ever again. I'd show him. I'd show her. I'd show them all.

I had literally been sitting on my sofa for days, simply clicking the TV channels back and forth. I hadn't moved, except to go to the bathroom, until my plan was ready to go. Today I had cleaned up, washed my hair, bathed, eaten, and I felt 100 percent better.

I always felt exhilarated when I knew I was about to handle anybody who stood in my path. My mama had taught me that, if nothing else. She had always said, "Don't you ever let anyone run over you. You hear me? Make them pay." That had become one of my mantras in life.

As I sipped on a glass of fresh lemonade, I thought back to how I made Michael pay back in L.A. I still couldn't believe I had trusted him enough to tell him my secrets. That was mistake number one, but it really didn't matter, because in the end he paid just like the others. In the end, he took my secrets to the grave. I remembered every detail; I always did.

Michael and I were in his king-sized bed. Thinking back, it seemed like we were always in bed, naked.

"Babe, do you trust me?" I asked, turning my body so I could stare into his masculine face.

"Of course I do. What kind of question is that?" Michael asked, basking in the afterglow of the great sex we had just experienced.

"What if I revealed something that changed your opinion of me?"

"That would never happen," he said, stroking the side of my face. I leaned into his large, warm hand.

I looked at him, wanting and needing to believe him so badly.

"Are you sure?"

"Pilar, what are you talking about? What's going on?" he asked, leaving a trail of kisses on my bare shoulders.

"What if I shared information about myself that showed me in a negative light? Would that change your opinion of me?"

"No, baby. I've already told you absolutely not."

I lay back down on my back, looked up at the ceiling, and sighed.

"What?" he asked.

It was now or never. "You know I love you, right?"

He nodded, looking at me curiously. I guess the reporter side of him came out.

"I hope we have a future together, because I love being with you. You make me so happy."

Michael didn't comment one way or the other.

"I would never do anything to hurt you, babe."

"Pilar, is there something you need to tell me? I'm listening."

I took a deep breath. "The movie, Diary of a Stalker—*"*

"Wow, here we go again. What is your obsession with that damn movie?"

"I'm Pilar."

"I know you are," he stated.

"No, babe, I'm that Pilar, the one portrayed in the movie."

Michael laughed, looked at me, and laughed some more. When he noticed I wasn't laughing, his demeanor quickly changed. "You're kidding, right?"

I shook my head from side to side, turning so I could watch the many expressions that crisscrossed his face in a matter of seconds.

"I knew you shared the name. It's not an uncommon name," he stated, talking more to himself than to me.

I didn't comment. Simply remained quiet as I watched him go down his checklist as to why I couldn't possibly be that Pilar.

"You don't look like the Pilar that was plastered all over the media a year or so ago," Michael stated, like he had finally found a flaw in my confession. "I followed that story. It was everywhere. You couldn't miss it."

"First of all, I was always covered up, and secondly, I've had some plastic surgery. I didn't want people to recognize me as that person—the so-called stalker."

"Wow! You are perfectly sane."

"Yeah, I would hope so."

"Wow."

"Is that all you can say?"

"You are serious, aren't you?" Michael asked, looking deep into my eyes. *"Yes, I am. Very."*

"Did you do all those horrible things to that writer?"

I looked at Michael like he was an alien from outer space with three heads and six eyes.

"What do you think?"

"I have never witnessed you acting like that crazed woman from the movie."

"Exactly. Xavier told his version of the events, not mine. We were in love until Kendall messed up everything."

"Wasn't that his fiancée?"

"She was, but then Xavier and I met and fell in love."

"What happened?"

"Everything went wrong, and I became the villain in his mind."

"Wow."

"You still love me?" I asked, holding my breath as I awaited his answer.

"Pilar, you know I care for you," he stated, pulling me close, burrowing his face into my hair. *"Let's talk about this later, because you have given me a lot to absorb."*

I instantly knew I had made a terrible mistake in telling him my true identity. I felt his body tense as he held me close, and I could feel his accelerated heartbeat. I noticed how he couldn't look directly into my eyes, and when I suggested we have sex again, suddenly he was too tired. When did that ever happen? Never.

A couple of days later I discovered Michael had pulled a background check on me, and then he gradually stopped coming by as often and didn't touch base with me throughout the day. Nor did he attempt to *sneak hugs and kisses behind closed doors when I came into his office. The most damning indicator was that he never asked any more questions. I knew curiosity had to be killing him. Plus, he was a reporter, it was in his blood, yet he barely asked any questions after my revelation, probably because he believed the events from the movie.*

I picked up on the lingering eye contact he gave to Sherry, the entertainment reporter, and I realized I was being replaced. If I was replaceable, then he had never loved me to begin with. That was a problem. A big one.

Later the headline read, EDITOR COMMITS SUICIDE, FOUND DEAD INSIDE CAR. *What a shame.*

Now sweet Kendall was about to find out I didn't play, either.

Chapter 24

Dre'

"Great. I'll see you in about an hour."

"See you soon," Milan said.

"Call if you get turned around."

"I will."

"You have the correct address, right?" I asked.

Milan laughed and read it back to me a second time.

"That's it. I've been looking forward to seeing you all week. Xavier thinks someone else is currently possessing my body."

"Why would he think that?" Milan asked.

I laughed. "It's a long story, but I'll explain when I see you. Drive carefully. The roads are still slick from the earlier rain."

I hung up, with a wide grin on my face and an excitement I hadn't experienced in a while. After two divorces, I almost felt giddy, like a teenager going on a first date with a girl he really liked. I really liked Milan. This would be the third date for us, and we had talked almost every day, except for when she traveled out of town for business.

Tonight, since she was going to be on my side of town, Milan suggested meeting at my home. I had yet to see her place, because for our last dinner date, she met me at the restaurant. She said she didn't want to inconvenience me. Milan was sweet like that.

I gave my living room a quick once-over with my eyes. I wouldn't want her to think I was a slob. I picked up a few sports and financial magazines and placed them in the magazine rack and put the glasses and plates on the coffee table in the dishwasher. Lastly, I checked out my bedroom, just in case, to make sure it was in order. Then I waited, impatiently.

When the doorbell chimed, I almost leapt from my seat. I crossed the few steps to the front door and eagerly opened it with a genuine smile.

"Hey," I said, pulling Milan in for a lingering hug. "It's good to see you."

"Hey, yourself," she said, kissing me on the cheek. "You smell good enough to eat."

"Thanks, and you have your hands full."

I backed up so Milan could enter.

"Let me give you a hand," I said, reaching for the grocery bag and the smaller bag she carried.

"Thanks. I hope you don't mind, but I had this great idea to fix dinner for you."

I'm sure I looked stunned for a few seconds, because the women I had dated in the past, well, it was all about them. Not a one had ever volunteered to do such a sweet thing. They weren't about to mess up their hair or nails by slaving over a hot stove. My exes were too busy making sure I made reservations at the most expensive restaurants in town to ever consider cooking.

"That is very sweet of you, and I appreciate it," I said, leading the way into the kitchen and placing the bags on the island.

"Wow. This is a beautiful kitchen," Milan said, taking it all in.

"Thank you, and by the way, you look beautiful tonight." Milan really was a gorgeous woman, with her smooth brown skin, long legs, sexy body, and those big, innocent eyes.

"Thank you, babe. You always know exactly what to say. If you don't mind, open that small bag and chill the bottle of red wine I picked up."

"Sure. Not a problem."

"Now, I need you to clear the kitchen and relax in the living room until I get dinner started," she said.

"You sure you don't need any help?"

"I got this. One thing I know, and that is my way around the kitchen. Go. Relax. Chill. Let me handle this. Let me take care of you."

An hour later, we sat down to wine, Parmesan cream sauce served over fettuccine, and a garden fresh salad. Milan had found some candles, and we ate by soft, shimmering candlelight. I turned on soft jazz, and the mood was set.

Milan anxiously watched as I took a few bites.

"Well, what do you think? You like?"

"I like a lot," I said, looking into her eyes.

I could have sworn she blushed.

"No, silly. I mean the food. Concentrate now. Is it all right?"

"It's delicious, baby."

"Good. Isn't this much better than going to a crowded, noisy restaurant and paying for overpriced, undercooked, underseasoned food?"

I nodded and took another bite that she held to my mouth with her fork.

"This way we can spend some quiet time together and get to know each other better," she added.

"I'd like that." I stared at Milan. In fact, I couldn't take my eyes off of her even if I'd wanted to. She captivated and mystified me at the same time.

"What?"

"Nothing. I was thinking how you are so different from most women I meet."

"I hope that's good." She looked at me questioningly.

"It's more than good."

"You know you have to explain yourself," she said, taking a sip of wine.

"I meet a lot of women who come at me from a monetary stance. I'm not rich, but I do well for myself. A lot of women think this means I'm supposed to take care of them financially."

"I've always believed in being independent and taking care of myself."

"That's a refreshing attitude." I took another bite. "This is good. What's in the sauce?"

"It's a secret family recipe. If I tell you, I'll have to kill you." She laughed.

"We wouldn't want that."

She didn't respond one way or the other.

Milan took a few more bites of her food. "How's your friend?"

"Xavier is doing fine. I really want you to meet him soon, and I've told him all about you."

I noticed Milan didn't comment, simply flashed a half smile.

I continued. "He's been through a lot, but I think I'm finally getting my old friend back."

"I take it that's good?"

"Of course. I was worried about him for a minute, because I thought he was going to turn into a recluse."

"Hmmm," she murmured, sipping more wine.

"All because of that bitch."

"Excuse me?" Milan shot back with a hint of anger in her tone.

I paused in mid-bite. "What did you say?" she asked, flashing a disgruntled look, which disappeared just as quickly as it had appeared.

"I'm sorry, Milan. Pardon my French. I still get angry when I think of all the things she subjected him to."

"More salad?" she asked, rising to place more on my plate with silver tongs.

"Just a little."

"Tell me when to stop."

"That's enough. That's good, baby."

"I'm sure your friend can handle himself. He certainly doesn't sound like a choirboy based on what you have told me."

"He's not, and I'm not saying he is—neither am I—but psycho Pilar fucked him up mentally and physically."

Again I noticed her wince with my choice of words.

"Listen, Milan, let's get something straight. I curse, probably more than I should, but I can't keep apologizing to you every time I say a four-letter word."

She remained silent. I couldn't tell if she was upset or if she was thinking about what I had said.

"This is who I am, and you have to take me or leave me, baby."

Milan didn't mutter a word. She simply scooted her chair back, got up, and seductively walked over to where I sat.

"I think I'll take you, then, with one condition."

"What is that?" I asked, pulling her onto my lap.

"You have to take me just as I am, too."

"It's a deal."

"We have to kiss on it to seal the deal," Milan stated.

"My pleasure," I said, leaning into her warm mouth, seeking out her tongue.

"Push your chair back and face me," Milan demanded, rising from my lap and standing patiently.

I did as she requested. Milan slowly bent down on her knees in front of me, unzipped the zipper to my pants, and pulled out my tool. I sat in amazement as she examined it, and it instantly grew in her hand.

"I love a man who's packing, babe. I can't wait to feel all that going up inside me."

"I hear you. I love when you talk dirty to me, baby."

"Do you want dessert?"

For once I was speechless. I could only nod my head like a little boy.

"Good, because I'm ready for some, too."

Milan stood up long enough to grab a can of whipped cream, syrup, and cherries out of the grocery bag that sat on the kitchen counter. Within minutes, she had made a chocolate sundae out of my dick. She added a couple of red cherries covered in whipped cream and proceeded to suck like she hadn't had a meal in days and was feasting on a banana split at Dairy Queen. I threw my head back, after saying a silent prayer to God, and couldn't believe my good fortune. She was a woman after my heart. She could cook and knew how to please her man. I couldn't wait to see what else Milan had up her sleeve.

Chapter 25

Xavier

As soon as I stepped into the foyer of my home and turned off my security alarm, I instantly sensed something wasn't quite right. I couldn't place my finger on it at that moment, but my senses were telling me something was amiss. The fine hairs on my arms were literally standing up at attention.

I had returned from three hours of writing at my favorite Starbucks. I hadn't gone out and written at a public venue in a while, mainly because I was now recognizable, and fans would come up and ask for an autograph or photo, or stare and point at me, or both. I always felt like I was on display. And let's not forget the aspiring writers who wanted advice, or wanted you to take a look at a manuscript they just happened to have with them. And then there were those who wanted to talk your ear off about how to get published yet hadn't written one single word. All of this was distracting when a writer was trying to get focused and drawn into his characters' thoughts, feelings, and actions. It seriously fucked up my creative flow.

Then, after the entire "Pilar, the Stalker" story broke, I simply didn't like the crowds, because I didn't know if they loved or hated me. I experienced both back then. There didn't appear to be an in-between. When the story first broke that a "bestselling author had assaulted his alleged mistress," all hell broke loose. Readers and book clubs boycotted my backlist titles, took sides, and assumed everything the media reported was fact. The media outlets had a field day reporting every little development.

I came across looking like the evil villain, while the mysterious Pilar was a victim of circumstance, taken advantage of by a womanizing man. That was such bullshit, but I was wading, almost drowning, waist deep in it back then.

Back at home, I wandered into the living room, where everything appeared to be in order. Near my staircase, I vaguely smelled a woman's perfume. The scent was light, soft, and flowery. I had smelled it before. It was the same fragrance Pilar wore. I looked around cautiously, searching out items, sounds, and movement within fifty feet of where I suddenly stood frozen.

I laughed out loud to myself when I caught my reflection in a large gold-plated mirror across from the stairs that led to a lower level. I looked frazzled and unnerved and frightened.

"This is fucking ridiculous. What am I doing? I'm letting my imagination get the better of me."

I shook my head and walked into the kitchen. I wasn't ready to venture upstairs, not just yet. Instead, I poured myself a glass of orange juice, gulped it down, and thought about how crazy I was acting. I was jumping at shadows and imagining phantom smells. Maybe I did need to talk with a professional.

After placing my empty glass in the sink, I slowly made my way upstairs and entered my bedroom, cautiously looked around. Nothing. All was quiet, and I exhaled, breathed a huge sigh of relief.

I took a few steps farther into my bedroom, and then I saw it. Was I being paranoid? There was a small dent in the comforter on the side of my bed, the side I slept on. It looked like someone had sat down on the edge; the comforter was dented in only one spot. I tried to think back. Did I sit back down on the bed after I made it up? I didn't think so. Plus, the imprint was small, more like one a woman would leave.

I literally stood staring at it for a bit longer, bugging out, willing it to go away. It didn't. I found myself slipping my hand under the mattress, searching. I was searching for underwear, women's panties, to be exact. When I was dealing with Pilar, she actually left a pair of her panties underneath my mattress and told my fiancée where to find them as proof that we had been sexing in my bed. Other than my countless lies, infidelity, and betrayal, Kendall finding the cum-stained panties was the last straw for her. The ironic thing was that I had never had sex with Pilar in *my* bed; she had deliberately planted the panties.

I finally convinced myself I had sat on the bed before I left for Starbucks. That had to be the only logical explanation. My house was locked up tighter than a maximum-security prison. There was no way in hell anyone could get in and out. The other alternative was something I didn't want to think about or even consider.

Earlier, after writing for a few hours at Starbucks, I decided to stop by Panera Bread for lunch before returning home. I had my usual sandwich and soup. I now felt the need to brush my teeth, and while I was thinking about it, a hot shower would be nice, too. I needed to clear my mind and refocus. I hated myself when I started thinking of Pilar out of the blue. I guessed now that I thought about it, it really wasn't randomly. My thoughts of her were always triggered by something—a smell, a laugh, a song, a woman's hairstyle or certain smile. At any time, any of those things took me back in time. Each time I would snap out of it a bit flustered by my reaction to the memory.

I strolled into the bathroom buck naked and stopped dead in my tracks. Lying on top of the counter, near the sink, was my toothbrush. There was no way in hell I left it out like that. First of all, I brushed my teeth that morning, and after finishing up, my normal routine was to rinse my toothbrush off and place it back in the toothbrush holder.

Think. Think. Think.

Was I distracted this morning? Did my cell ring? Did anything happen to make me forget to put it back?

Oh, yeah. Dre' called to tell me about his date. I swear the man had reverted to a lovesick teenager. This woman, this Milan, had his nose wide open. I had known Dre' all my life, had survived marriages and breakups right beside him, and I had never seen him this infatuated.

I turned on the shower and adjusted the water to as hot as I could take it. I slipped in and lathered up my washcloth with my favorite shower gel and submerged my face underneath the water. I was pleased that the mystery had been solved, and I took my time with my shower. I enjoyed the feel of the hot water coursing down my tense body, combined with the exotic, musky smell of the shower gel. Kendall had gotten me into using this product, and now I couldn't go without it. Plus, the smell of it brought back memories of Kendall and me making love in the shower on numerous occasions.

Just as I turned off the water, stepped out, and reached for my towel, it hit me. Dre' did call, but I picked up the call as I was walking down the steps. There was no way I was distracted in the bathroom.

All thoughts of the mysterious toothbrush dissipated when I heard the familiar sound indicating I had a text message.

Hi. Just wanted to say hello. Hope your day is going well.

Still in the nude, I quickly texted back.
Kendall, what are you doing?

Nothing. Just seeing how you were doing. Talk soon.

I walked downstairs, with an even bigger mystery to solve. What was going on with Kendall? She had made it perfectly clear at our lunch that she was happily married. She had accepted my apology, received her closure, and lunch had ended with her moving on to live her life happily ever after. I was to live my own life, separate from and independent of hers. End of story.

Now I had received this text. Kendall wasn't the type to sneak around. Her commitments were strong and true. She had dumped me like a hot potato once she found out I had cheated on her. Could she possibly want me back, or was the good doctor not throwing down the way she had grown accustomed to with me? All these questions and many more bombarded my thoughts. If I hadn't been so occupied with thoughts of Kendall, I would have noticed the clothes hanger in the back of my closet suddenly swinging back and forth. I also might have noticed the dark shadow as it silently crept beneath my bed to lie in wait until nighttime fell hours later—lying beneath me as I slept unknowingly throughout the night.

Chapter 26

Kendall

Kendall casually strolled to her silver metallic Mercedes in the covered parking garage. Life was good. She had a wonderful, successful husband who doted on her and answered to her every whim. She had a great budding career as an attorney, one she had always dreamed of; and she lived in the home of her childhood dreams, in an exclusive neighborhood; and, well, yes, life was good.

The only thing missing, she couldn't have, or could she? Kendall pondered that question as she pushed the UNLOCK button on the key to her luxury car. She had had a good workout with her personal trainer, Phil. He was tough, always pushing her to reach her full potential. She hated him sometimes, but he was one of the best, and she could afford the best. Kendall realized most people who knew her viewed her as a diva. She accepted the title as an honor. There was nothing wrong with wanting the best life had to offer.

Kendall hummed an unrecognizable tune and smiled to herself as she closed the distance to her car. She still couldn't believe she had sent a text to Xavier. She didn't know what she was thinking, but she definitely realized what the consequences would be if her husband ever found out. Kendall knew this was totally out of character for her, but seeing Xavier again had confused her.

Seeing Xavier had unleashed a desire that shocked her with its strength.

Could she have it all? Was it possible to have a great career, a fabulous house, a wealthy husband, and a skilled lover on the side? She didn't even know, didn't know if she was willing to go that far to find out. For now, she simply knew she had to see Xavier again. Seeing him at the restaurant had brought back feelings she thought were under wraps.

As soon as she climbed behind the wheel and locked her door, she felt his presence before she actually saw him. She instantly froze with fright.

"If you know what's good for you, I wouldn't turn around, Kendall," the male presence in the backseat stated in a frightening, calm voice. This was right before he placed a huge steel knife tip against the artery of her neck. He wasn't nervous or in a hurry. She reasoned that this wasn't new to him.

"How do you know my name?" she asked. Looking back later, she would think, *What a silly question to ask.*

"It doesn't matter. Let's just say we have a mutual acquaintance."

"What do you want? Please don't hurt me. I have money. Credit cards. They're in my purse. Take it. Take all of it," she said, attempting to turn around, fumbling with her oversize bag.

"Didn't I tell you not to turn around? Seeing my face would be a huge mistake," he screamed, pushing the tip of the blade deeper into her fragile neck, near the pulsating vein.

Kendall silently commanded herself to remain calm. For some reason, she felt a need to keep him talking. Focusing in front of her, she tried to determine if there was an escape route. She knew from statistics that she couldn't drive away with him. Even if she had to crash the car, she couldn't allow him to take her from this location. Kendall looked around to see if anyone was in the parking garage, someone she could scream to for help. She wondered if she could outrun him; it would take only a second to open the car door and jump out. Her eyes traveled to the car horn, inches from her fingers.

As if sensing her next move, the dark presence said, in a chilling voice, "If you blow that horn, bitch, that'll be the last thing you do. I guarantee it. Do you understand, bitch?"

Kendall frantically nodded and tried her best to will the tears from forming. She had to remain calm and remember the details. She couldn't get emotional and weak.

"What do you want from me? My husband is expecting me, and if I don't arrive home soon, he'll come looking for me. He knows I'm here."

"I have a message to deliver."

"What? A message? From who?" she muttered behind tears that threatened to spill.

"You don't need to know all that. You need to shut up, listen, and listen good."

"Okay."

"Stay the fuck away from Xavier Preston."

"What?"

"You heard me the first time, bitch. Stay away from him. Don't call him. Don't text him. Don't meet him for lunch. Stay away. Plain and simple."

She was shocked into silence. It was apparent someone had been watching her. Chills instantly went up and down her spine. She was angry at herself for putting herself in this position by meeting with Xavier. She should have followed her first instinct and let it be.

"You wouldn't want your surgeon hubby to find out you're trying to seek out some new dick, would you?"

"Don't," she said, pulling away from his thick fingers, fingers that were now feeling her up, caressing her breasts and nipples through the sheer fabric of her workout outfit. "No."

"What? I'm not good enough to touch you?" He laughed. "Stuck-up bitch."

"Please, stop!"

"Hmmm, you smell good," he said, leaning his nose into her hair. "Good enough to eat."

With those words, he felt her body stiffen. He managed to get her sports bra unsnapped and now freely tweaked her nipples and played with her breasts.

Kendall started to cry, making whimpering sounds.

"Is this what you wanted that nigga Xavier to do to you?" he asked, leaning forward as his right hand traveled to a place between her legs. He had moved the knife to his left hand, the tip still against her tender neck. He kissed her neck and ran his thick, moist tongue over her ear, sticking the tip in and making wet, icky sounds.

"I asked you a question, bitch. Is this what you wanted?"

She frantically shook her head from side to side.

He laughed a bitter, cruel, evil laugh. "I believe you're lying. You were going to give him some pussy while your poor husband was operating on a poor soul, none the wiser."

Kendall whimpered louder, not believing this was happening to her. A scream was stuck deep in her throat.

"Shhh. Isn't that right? Open your legs, bitch. Wider."

Kendall slowly obliged, with help from the male presence. He stuck his entire hand down her pants and pushed her thong aside and then drove two fingers deep into her womanhood.

"Damn. You are about to make me bust a nut up in here. I have never played in any rich pussy before. Ohhh, you feel good," he said, breathing heavily now and talking in a raspy voice that made her cringe with disgust.

Kendall, despite her best effort, couldn't recoil far enough from his touch.

"Keep those legs wide open, or I'll cut that pretty face up so good that no one will recognize you, not even your own mama."

She placed her hand over her mouth to keep from screaming as he eagerly went in and out of her with his thick fingers. He didn't show any mercy.

"Tell me it feels good."

She hesitated.

"Say it, bitch."

"It feels good," she spat between clenched teeth.

"Good girl. Now, what are you supposed to do so I won't have to pay you another visit? Because make no mistake, I will. And next time, you best believe it won't be my fingers up in that sweet stuff. You ain't ever been with a real nigga before, and it would be my pleasure to teach you the ropes and break you in," he said, moving his finger in and out of her ever so slowly. He was enjoying her distress.

"Stay away from Xavier," she managed to whisper.

"Good girl. What else?" he asked, breathing heavily down her neck, still fingering her.

Kendall tensed again, looking confused.

"You are not to tell anyone about this conversation. That means the police, Xavier, and the good surgeon. Understand?"

"Yes," she said, barely audible.

"I can't hear you, bitch."

Kendall nodded.

"I need to hear you say it so I can be clear that we have an understanding."

"Yes."

"Hmmm, you feel so damn good. Look at you. Getting all wet. See, I knew you liked me. Bounce up and down on my fingers."

Kendall hesitated, and he pressed the tip of the knife deeper.

"That's it. Act like those fingers are your husband's dick or, better yet, Xavier's. You are one lucky bitch, because if I didn't have you out here, you would definitely be getting a taste of my dick. I'd be tearing up that stuff right about now."

"Please stop!"

He whispered into her ear. "Remember, I know everything about you. I know where you live, work, and even where you go to church. Go back to being a faithful, good Christian wife and live happily after ever. That way you never have to see me again."

He thrust his meaty fingers into her a few more times; it was obvious he was deriving great pleasure out of the entire situation, her discomfort and terror.

"Moan for me."

Kendall proceeded to moan as he slowly pulled his fingers out of her. To her surprise, he reached around the back of her and stuck a finger into her anus.

"Ahhh," she screamed as he inserted it back and forth, again and again, stretching it open.

"Shut up. Grab that wheel with your hands, lean over, and push that ass up. You blow that horn, I'll hurt you. Hurt you bad."

"Please don't! Stop!"

"Now!"

Kendall did as he commanded.

She leaned over, raised her ass from the seat, and he snatched her pants down, along with her thong. He continued to assault her anus with his finger and then another finger.

"That's definitely a virgin hole. Tight. Tight. Tight. Moan, bitch," he said, smacking the back of her ass with his rough, callous hand a couple of times.

In between cries, she moaned for him. He had the nerve to lay the knife on the seat beside him, knowing she was too afraid to do anything foolish by this time. He had a finger of his right hand inserted in her vagina, and a finger of his left inside her anus, moving them simultaneously. Occasionally, he'd take his finger out of her anus to squeeze her nipples until she cried out in pain. She knew he enjoyed her pain, got off on it. She also knew he was capable of anything.

Suddenly, as quickly as it had started, he pulled away and opened the back door without warning.

"Remember what I said. Don't be stupid. You have been warned."

With that he was gone in a flash. The entire incident had lasted less than fifteen minutes. Kendall pulled her pants back up, rested her head against the steering wheel, and bawled like a baby. Much later, she composed herself enough to drive home. With shaky hands, she turned on the engine, placed it in drive, and drove away. Besides being afraid, she knew she could never tell anyone about what happened, especially not her new husband.

Chapter 27

Dre'

After a stressful day at work, I couldn't wait to arrive home so I could relax with a beer and chill out with one of the *CSI* shows I watched religiously.

It had been a few days since Milan and I had gone out, or should I say, stayed in. That night, after she prepared a delicious home-cooked meal, the date ended with a bang. I still had flashbacks of what she did to me. Whew!

I unlocked the front door and walked in, tossing the mail I had picked up outside on the marble table that sat in the foyer. My nose was immediately assaulted by various mouthwatering smells, which instantly brought on a stomach growl. I didn't realize how hungry I was until that very moment. I had worked through lunch.

I walked farther into the living room and looked around curiously. Everything was spotless and smelling like cleaning products. I would admit, I was not the tidiest guy around. After all, I was a bachelor and lived by myself. If I liked my clutter and I was comfortable with it, then it was no one else's business.

Magazines, newspapers, glasses, and dirty dinner plates were no longer strewn around the living room coffee table. I ate a lot of takeout and rarely used my kitchen table. Most evenings found me camped out in front of the TV, going over reports from work and watching TV as I ate. Most nights I was too tired or too lazy to carry my clutter into the kitchen, but I made a point of loading the dishwasher at least once a week.

There was no evidence of that now. I looked down at my feet. The carpet looked freshly vacuumed, and the pillows on my sofa were sitting high and were fluffed up. I smelled a faint floral scent, which clung to the air and teased my nose in a pleasing way.

When I walked into the kitchen, to my surprise and amazement, I found a full meal waiting on the stove. A place at the dining table had been set, complete with a place mat, flatware, a dinner plate, and a glass. When I opened the large black pot on the stove and peeked inside, I found meaty stew, and thick, crusty bread sat on the counter, along with a vase of fresh flowers and a handwritten note.

> *Hi, babe,*
> *I know you work hard, so I decided to do some-*
> *thing extra special for you. You deserve this and*
> *much more. Enjoy. Oh, by the way, I'll have des-*
> *sert for you this weekend. It starts with a naked*
> *Milan, a few adult toys, and you.*
> *I miss you.*
> *Hugs and kisses*

I couldn't believe Milan had gone through that much trouble. I still hadn't figured out how she had gotten into my home. So far she was batting one thousand in my book. One, she could cook. Two, she could clean. Three, she could throw down in the bedroom. And four, she was sweet and intelligent. What more could a man ask for? I couldn't wait for her and Xavier to meet, the two most important people in my life, other than my recovering alcoholic mother. Once Milan found out

I was friends with a celebrity, she couldn't stop asking questions about Xavier. Her curiosity had really been piqued, because Xavier's name always seemed to come up in conversation.

After I finished my meal and had second helpings, I finally made it upstairs to my bedroom. Milan had hooked it up with surprises, too. She had a fresh pair of tan drawstring pajamas laid out on the bed, next to a single red rose and another note. It read:

> *Babe,*
> *I loved how you made me feel the other night. You are super sexy.*
> *Check your e-mail. I sent you a video of me in a rather compromising position.*
> *Hugs and kisses*

After reading the note, I rushed to my laptop, and sure enough, there was an e-mail attachment with Milan getting herself off in full view of the camera. Her top was off as she rubbed some sort of oil on her breasts in slow, circular motions, until her nipples were taut and erect. Then she edged her fingers down to her lower body. She had on a sexy black thong, which she slowly inched out of, and proceeded to open herself up wide.

As she played with her womanhood, I found my dick growing hard. Milan was hot and wet, her juices on her fingers. She took her time teasing me. She zoomed in, up close, and I realized she was coming as her body started to shake and tremble with a tremendous force. My only regret was that she never showed her lovely face; however, I would know that sexy body anywhere.

After viewing the steamy video, I was ready for a very cold shower. To my surprise, she had placed new bottles of body gel on the countertop, and her lips were outlined in red lipstick on my vanity mirror. I took a somewhat cold shower as I replayed the video in my mind. It never crossed my mind again that I had never given Milan a key to my home. Later she would explain that she had talked my elderly neighbor, the one who had a spare key, courtesy of me, into letting her in.

Chapter 28

Xavier

I was chilling in the living room at Dre's house, in front of his big-screen TV, with a cold beer in one hand and chips in the other. We were watching the game, and it was now halftime.

"I'm telling you, man, that something isn't right. I just can't put my finger on it," I said in between crunchy bites.

"You said yourself that your imagination has been playing tricks on you lately. I guess that's one of the hazards of being a writer."

I finished dipping my tostada chip in the spicy salsa that sat on the coffee table, in a nearly empty ceramic bowl. "Man, I'm pretty sure I didn't leave my toothbrush lying on the countertop. I never do that . . . ever. People are creatures of habit, and I know myself."

Dre' looked curiously at me. "But you aren't a hundred percent certain?"

"No, not one hundred percent."

He gave me a look that said, "Well, that explains it."

I delved further to plead my case. I was desperate for someone to believe me and confirm I wasn't going crazy. "Remember what I told you my assistant, Khai, confided about being afraid to be alone in the house?"

"You've spooked her with your crazy talk. That's all."

"How do you explain the perfume smell I sniffed the moment I opened the front door?" I asked, throwing up my hands. "Damn, I don't wear perfume, and if I ever start, check me in for the mandatory forty-eight hours of observation at the nearest loony bin."

"Hell, I don't know how to explain it. I'm not a psychologist."

"It's like that. Are you suggesting that I need help?"

"No, no, I'm not saying that. I just think it wouldn't hurt for you to talk to someone. To talk through all you've been through lately. Everybody handles stress in different ways. It doesn't mean you are weak, man."

I didn't respond. Just took a big salsa-covered chip and tossed it whole in my mouth.

"You know what I'm saying?"

"You are serious, aren't you?" I replied.

He didn't respond, and that confirmed his answer.

"Of all the ladies' perfume fragrances, I smelled the one Pilar wore religiously."

"Seriously, Xavier, our minds can play tricks on us. Wasn't your home locked up and secure?" Dre' asked matter-of-factly.

I hesitated, knowing what he was implying. "Yes."

"Do you really think someone broke in and then locked back up?"

"That's the problem. I don't know what to think anymore."

"Everything you have told me has a reasonable explanation. The indentation on the bedspread was a case of you sitting on the edge of the bed, and not remembering, or not making the bed up properly."

"Dre', it was an ass print, and it wasn't mine," I stated, raising my voice an octave higher as I spoke.

I saw him check me out from the corner of his eye.

I lowered my voice. I was very aware that I was coming across as paranoid. "Plus, I told you I've had a few voice mails that I never received. They mysteriously disappeared."

"How do you know you missed them, then?" Dre' questioned, still playing devil's advocate as he took a swig of beer.

"Because the person, sometimes my agent, would ask me about it later. Like 'Why didn't you call me back?' or 'Didn't you get my message?' It couldn't be any plainer than that."

"Maybe the person didn't leave the message the proper way."

"Damn, man, it's not rocket science."

"I don't know what to tell you. What do you feel is going on?"

I looked at the TV commercial currently playing and didn't respond right away. I knew my theory would sound absolutely ludicrous. I hesitated.

"Well?"

"Man, I don't know. Some weird shit has been crossing my mind. What if it's Pilar?"

Dre' had just taken a swig of his beer and almost choked in laughter. "I know you are kidding. Please tell me you are kidding. Pilar?"

"What's so unbelievable about that?" I asked, feeling a bit upset that he thought my explanation was so far-fetched.

"Xavier, that psycho is long gone. She finally figured out you didn't want her loony ass, and besides, she would be a fool to come back after the scrutiny the media placed on your lives the last time. She may have been crazy, but she wasn't stupid."

"Gone where, though?"

"I couldn't tell you. She went back to where crazy people reside, somewhere in Crazyland, USA."

"What if she is back, somewhere right here in Houston?"

"Have you seen her?"

"No."

"Have you talked to her?"

"No."

"Have you received any mysterious phone hang-ups, had your tires slashed, or received any dead roses?"

"No, I haven't, but that doesn't mean anything."

"Yes, it does. That was her MO. Listen to yourself and how paranoid you sound."

"I don't think so."

"Just don't find yourself alone with Pilar in a hotel room again and you'll be fine."

"Man, that's not funny," I said.

"Xavier, it really is. I'm sorry, but it was. You didn't see yourself wrapped up in that sheet, looking like black Jesus, after Pilar literally whipped your ass with that leather whip. She did everything but carve her name in your chest."

"And I'll go to my grave with you reminding me."

"And you know it." He laughed at that.

"Forget it."

"Maybe you do need to start writing another book. You have too much time on your hands in that big-ass house you own."

"I have already started outlining a story line."

"I can't believe I'm saying this, but good for you. I would say you need to take some time to relax, but writing flows through your veins like blood. That's your lifeline, and you wouldn't be happy without it. Your two favorite things in the world are writing and pussy."

"I'm surprised I even received an invite to come over today. You have been hanging so tight with your new woman that you are ghost most of the time."

That got a genuine smile out of Dre'.

"Yeah, we have been spending a lot of time together. I admit, I like her a lot. I even gave her a key to my place."

"You what?" I asked, nearly choking on my beer.

"You heard right."

"What's next? The two of you moving in together?"

"Maybe."

I looked over at him, and he wasn't joking. "Wow. I have to definitely meet this chick. She must be putting it on you good."

"No comment, but you will meet her soon."

"What? No comment about her sexing skills. I know I can't wait to meet her now, and I'm definitely holding you to that."

"You mentioned you had to tell me something about Kendall," Dre' said.

"I do, but it can wait. The game is back on, but remind me to tell you later."

"You just get ready to pay my one hundred dollars, and I want it before you walk out the door. No rain checks," Dre' stated.

Chapter 29

Pilar

That's what I'm talking about. Now you are acting like my daughter, my mother's voice echoed in my head. *You showed that bitch.* I shook my head and rubbed my temples to quiet the ugly, disgusting voice. I hated her as much as I hated Kendall. I was happy she was dead and rotting in hell, exactly where she deserved to be.

Suddenly uncontrollable laughter overtook me. I laughed so hard and so long that tears streamed down my cheeks and my stomach ached as my entire body shook. Every time I thought I had it under control, the laughter would start up again.

According to my source, Kendall was scared shitless and wouldn't be going within two inches of Xavier, now or ever again. She wouldn't forget this lesson anytime soon. I also heard during my debriefing from my source that he had checked out the goodies. I didn't tell him to do all that, but it didn't make a difference one way or the other to me. Neither Kendall nor Bailey was going to get in the way of my grand plan. Casualties were simply a tragedy of war.

The best part of all was that Xavier didn't suspect a thing. If he did, he couldn't prove it. I had been extra careful in my comings and goings. I was going to teach Xavier Preston a lesson he wouldn't soon forget. I was going to teach him once and for all that he couldn't fuck with me. What did Kendall and Bailey have that I didn't have? I would make him pay. I'd make them all pay. Xavier thought he had seen the last of me, but I didn't give up that easily.

Sure I had gone away for a year to a lush tropical island. It was during that time that I received my plastic surgery, recovered, and recouped from the media frenzy that took place in the United States. I loved it there, and for a brief period of time, I was at peace.

I was willing to wait. Wait on Xavier. I knew with all my heart he would come to his senses and realize we were meant to be together. Xavier was my soul mate, and no one could tell me any differently. I knew what I felt in my heart. I came back to the States a new and improved person. I was rested and confident again. Leeda, my one true friend, had gotten me back on my meds, and we talked at least once a week. Life was looking good again, not like an ugly, endless, empty sea of murkiness.

To my surprise, I was able to get a job rather quickly, doing something I was good at. Of course, Michael was an added bonus. Initially, he was going to be someone to spend time with until Xavier came to his senses, but soon I developed feelings for him and thought that maybe it was possible to have two very different soul mates. Anything was possible.

Then the betrayal happened, by both Xavier and Michael. Xavier put out that damn movie portraying me as an evil, deranged stalker, and Michael betrayed me by pulling away from the relationship we had established. Both betrayals boiled down to lies, lies, lies, and more lies. I couldn't let them continue to hurt me. If you crossed me, I struck out with a vengeance. Maybe I was my mother's daughter.

I relaxed on the sofa and thought about how easy it was to come and go in Xavier's home. He thought he was so smart. Well, I was smarter. I admit, he almost caught me a few days ago. To my surprise, because he was usually such a routine-based person, he arrived home earlier than I had anticipated. Prior to him arriving, I hadn't been doing much. Most times I wandered from room to room, admiring his fabulous home. For a man, Xavier had good taste. Sometimes, I would read portions of the manuscript he was working on, or I would take a nap in his bed and imagine him lying beside me, holding me close. I would hold his pillow close, pretend it was him, and inhale his scent. Usually, I would make a sandwich or drink bottled water, and occasionally, I would even watch a little TV or view a movie from his extensive collection.

The day Xavier came home early, I was lucky I heard the alarm being disarmed. It gave me enough time to quickly walk upstairs without being seen. I secretly watched him as he walked from room to room. I think he even drank a glass of orange juice. As he made his way upstairs, thirty minutes later, I rushed to hide in his gigantic walk-in bedroom closet. He didn't have a clue I was there.

I intensely watched him through a crack in the door as he came into the master bedroom. It took all I had not to reveal myself to him. Xavier was such a handsome man, and the problem was that he knew it with every fiber of his being. The arrogant motherfucker. He was tall and dark and fine. Xavier had the cutest dimples and the sexiest smile. When he smiled, my world simply lit up. And he gave the best dick I had ever had. I knew if he apologized, I'd still take him back, but he hadn't apologized. So for now, I had to do what I had to do.

I waited patiently and felt myself getting wet as he stripped down to nothing as he prepared to take a shower. He had the body of a god, a work of art, and I knew very well that he definitely knew how to use what hung, thick and long, between his legs. I shook off flashbacks of him on top of me, inside me. He would take all he wanted, with my legs spread open, as he whispered naughty words that made me wetter. I shuddered and slightly parted my lips to release a soft moan. He was the best I had ever had. Unfortunately, he used and abused me and then tossed me away like a bag of trash filled with squirming maggots.

I stayed hidden in the closet, cherished every moment of simply being in his presence. It was as close to heaven as I had been in a while. Minutes later, when he turned off the shower and I heard him stepping out of the stall, I made my way over to his massive four-poster mahogany bed and climbed quietly and effortlessly beneath. There was more than enough room for me to recline comfortably, and I had the luxury of taking a nap with Xavier not being aware of me.

Later that night, once he climbed in bed, I reveled in being so close, so near to him. Just the knowledge that he was only inches above where I lay brought me ecstasy. I closed my eyes as an orgasm coursed through my trembling body. It was still fresh in my memory bank how, not too long ago, he was hoisted on two hands above my body as he pumped in and out of my spread legs with a savage fury and whispered naughty words into my ear. Every creak and groan of the mattress as he moved around brought me joy because I was in Xavier's space once again. Once he was lightly snoring, I reached up to touch the outline of his body through the mattress. I shivered as I imagined I was touching the real thing: his back, his chest, his manhood.

When I was pretty sure he was in the deep throes of sleep, I slowly, ever so quietly inched my way from beneath the bed. Xavier lay on his back with his legs spread wide and his covers tangled at his feet. I couldn't help but smile with the knowledge that he still slept the same way, all over the place. I stood to the left of him for a few minutes, simply basking in his presence.

When he was sleeping, I realized why I loved him so. I slowly circled the massive bed like a vulture circling its prey, never taking my eyes off him, and came around to his right side. I saw his eyes flutter, and he turned, so I instantly froze in mid-step, but then he went just as quickly into his familiar rhythm of breathing. I was towering above him. I lowered the back side of my hand and just barely caressed his cheek. I was so close that I could feel the heat radiating from his skin, and I couldn't help but lean down to smell the masculine scent that was him. Xavier was my God. My entire world began, centered, and ended around him.

I didn't rush my steps; I had all night, and the night was still young. I silently, like a creature of the darkness, slinked into a leather wing chair that sat in the far corner of the bedroom, in the shadows. I watched him sleep through the early morning hours, not once removing my eyes from him. Each moan, each turn, each twist of his athletic body, I observed as I breathed in his same air. During the wee hours, right before the sun rose to a new day, I let myself out, but not before tucking the covers back around him and blowing a sweet kiss his way as I walked out the bedroom door and down the stairs.

I realized he would find the items I had intentionally left for him to discover. I wanted to rattle him, play mental games with him. I wanted him to suffer, like he had made me suffer. Oh, we were just beginning.

Xavier hadn't seen anything yet. The question was, was he ready? He wouldn't or couldn't believe in a million years what I had in store for poor, pussy-whipped Dre'. This was going to be fun.

Let the games begin.

Chapter 30

Dre'

"Baby, I'm glad you don't mind that we aren't going out tonight," I said, placing a movie into the DVD player.

"Dre', you know that doesn't mean anything to me. I just enjoy spending time with you," Milan stated, snuggling up to me on the sofa now that the dinner dishes had been washed and put away. "It doesn't matter where we are."

"I promise I'll make it up to you," I said, wincing slightly.

"What's wrong, babe?" Milan questioned, closely studying my face.

"Nothing. I think I have a slight case of indigestion. I'll take a couple of Tums and will be good as new."

"What are you trying to say? You don't like my cooking," Milan said jokingly.

"Baby, you know I love your cooking, and I absolutely adore you," I said, pulling her closer.

"You are so sweet, and I never would have thought it."

"Wait. Hold up. I don't know how to take that. Is that a compliment or a dig?" I asked.

"No. I mean from outside appearances you come across as no-nonsense—tough."

"I am tough. Don't you know I'm from the hood?" I teased.

Milan laughed that laugh that I loved. Her face simply lit up like Christmas lights when she was happy. I noticed sometimes, when she didn't think I was watching, there was such a deep sadness. My goal was to make her smile and giggle and be happy.

"You are so silly."

"Seriously, I guess I know what you are saying," I stated.

"You don't act anything like Xavier. He's such a womanizer and sounds so full of himself. I despise men like him. They are so superficial and self-absorbed. Heaven and earth don't move when they enter a room and flash a smile. And all these stupid women oohing and aahing, pumping up their egos, hanging on their every word like they are Moses writing on the stone tablets, doesn't make matters better."

"Wow. I can't believe you are talking about my friend like that. He's not like you describe him at all. Baby, you have to get to know him before you jump to preconceived conclusions."

"I'm sorry. That's the way you make him sound."

"He does date a lot of women, but why shouldn't he? He's single and free. As long as he keeps it real and adult and mature, no one gets hurt. What's wrong with that?"

"People do get hurt, and that's a very real problem in my book."

I paused and looked at Milan curiously, because she sounded extremely passionate in making her point, as if she was taking it personally.

"From what you've told me, Pilar was hurt."

"Pilar was crazy," I stated simply.

"Why don't you stop saying that?" she asked, with a hint of anger in her voice that came out of nowhere.

"She was. Pilar was a straight-up psychotic, crazy-ass lunatic."

"You never know what drives a person to become the person they are. Everyone doesn't have a perfect childhood, so you shouldn't be so judgmental."

"I agree. Hell, my childhood wasn't peachy keen, either, because I sure as hell didn't grow up with a silver spoon in my mouth. But crazy is as crazy does, and I call them as I see them."

"Me too," she barely whispered.

"Huh?"

"Nothing, babe. Nothing at all. Forget it."

When I reached for her, to pull her closer, I felt her body stiffen.

"Quit pouting," I joked, looking down at her.

"I'm not."

"Yes, you are. We can agree to disagree," I said, placing a light kiss on her lips.

"Sure, I agree. Now, let's drop it and watch the movie," Milan stated.

I kissed her on the cheek, tickled her side, and smiled.

"What?"

"Do you know how much you mean to me? I can't imagine life without you now. Girl, you have me all sprung like mattress coils."

"You are silly."

"I'm glad you accepted the key to my house. I want you to come and go as you please, because I do understand you need your space as well. I enjoy coming home from work and having you here, though."

"And in the kitchen?" she joked.

"Yeah, but mostly in the bedroom," I said, gently kissing her neck. "You are so sexy. You know that?"

"Stop," she said, gently pulling away. "Let's watch the movie. We can save that for later. We have plenty of time."

An hour into the movie, my cell phone rang. I picked it up as Milan continued to watch the sappy romance she had chosen about finding your soul mate in life. Personally, I thought that concept was a pile of bull, but I didn't tell her that.

"What's up, man?" Xavier asked.

"Watching a movie with Milan."

"How sweet."

I laughed because Xavier was always getting on my case about how much time Milan and I spent together.

"Why? What's up?"

"I'm about three blocks from your house, and I was going to drop by, but I didn't know you had company."

"Stop by, anyway."

"Are you sure?" he asked. "I wouldn't want to interrupt anything."

"I'm positive. It's about time you and Milan met. In fact, we were just talking about you."

I noticed Milan had stopped watching the movie and was now anxiously staring at me.

"Okay, cool. See you in a few minutes."

Milan didn't waste a second when I hung up the phone.

"What's up, babe?"

"That was Xavier. He's in the area, and I asked him to stop by."

"You what?" she asked, turning so she was looking directly at me. For a brief moment, I thought I saw panic cross her face.

"He's going to stop by for a minute. This will give you and him an opportunity to finally meet."

She didn't respond.

"I hope you don't mind."

"Sure," was all she said.

Milan continued to sit on the sofa for a few minutes, pretending to watch the movie. I could tell she wasn't as into it as she was before.

"What's wrong?" I asked after observing her for a few minutes.

"Nothing. Why?"

"You seem antsy all of a sudden."

"I don't feel good. My stomach feels really queasy," she said, clutching it with the palm of her right hand and gently rubbing.

"I have more Tums. Do you want a couple?"

"No, I'll be okay. Just give me a few minutes."

About fifteen minutes later my doorbell rang, and I thought Milan would jump through the ceiling. She literally froze, like she was caught in the headlights of a fast-moving car.

"That must be Xavier," I said. "Are you all right? You don't have to be nervous about meeting him. He'll like you just as much as I adore you."

I got up to open the door and looked back at her as I made my way across the room.

She nodded her head and managed a slight smile.

It took just a few seconds to walk to the front door and let Xavier in, but when I turned around again, Milan was gone.

"Milan," I called, walking back into the sunken living room with Xavier. "She must have gone to the bathroom," I said to Xavier, who was walking behind me. "She was on the sofa a second ago, anxious to meet you. Grab a beer in the fridge. I'll be right back."

"Take your time, but tell Milan I can't wait to meet the woman who has domesticated your ass."

I walked to the bathroom, the one downstairs, which was typically reserved for guests. I called out to Milan but didn't receive a response. Finally, I ventured upstairs and found the bathroom door in my master bedroom closed. I walked to the door and could have sworn I heard Milan arguing with someone. I definitely heard more than one voice.

"Milan?" I called out, knocking on the door.

Suddenly the noise ceased. "Yes," she said, sounding very sick and weak.

"Are you okay?"

"No, I'm not. I just threw up dinner, and my head is pounding like someone is hitting it with a sledgehammer. I think I feel a migraine coming on."

"Poor baby. Do you need anything? What can I do?"

"No. Just give me a few minutes."

As I walked away, I heard vomiting sounds coming from behind the closed door. I walked back downstairs to find Xavier catching the last half of the movie we had been watching.

"Everything all right?" he asked, looking back at me.

"Yeah, I guess."

"Where's Milan?"

"Upstairs, with her head buried in the toilet, vomiting."

"That doesn't sound good. Maybe she has that stomach virus that's going around."

"Earlier my stomach was upset, and now Milan suddenly gets sick. Maybe it was something we ate or the bug you mentioned."

"Well, I hope she feels better." Pointing to the TV set, he said, "I didn't picture you as the sappy romantic guy."

"And you'd be correct. Milan is the romantic, so I have to please my woman."

"You have to please her now?" He laughed.

"Man, you know what I mean. Don't start."

Xavier and I talked for another thirty minutes or so, and Milan still hadn't made her way back downstairs. My eyes continued to wander to the stairway; it was obvious I was not into the conversation. Finally, Xavier got fed up with my lack of attention.

"Dre', go. Go check on your woman. I'm out of here, anyway."

"Man, you don't have to leave."

"I can sit at home and talk to myself. That's basically what I'm getting here."

I laughed. "She has been in the bathroom for a while now. I just want to make sure she's all right."

Xavier gulped down the last of his beer and got up to leave. "I'll holla at you tomorrow. We have to meet for b-ball soon so I can whup up on that ass."

"I was thinking the same thing, except you would be on the end of the whup ass."

"In your dreams. Tell Milan I said hello, and maybe we'll have the opportunity to meet soon, because I have the impression she is not going anywhere if you have your way."

"I'll tell her."

"Again, I hope she feels better."

"Thanks, man."

"Peace. I'm out."

I locked the door behind Xavier and almost sprinted up the stairs, two at a time. When I entered the bathroom, Milan was washing her flushed face and getting ready to brush her teeth with the extra toothbrush she kept at my house.

"Feeling better?" I asked, pulling her into my arms and nuzzling her neck.

"I'm feeling a little better now. Let's go meet your friend," she said softly.

"Xavier is gone. He just left."

"You're kidding. I was looking forward to meeting him."

"There will be other times for that. He said for you to feel better."

"Thanks. That was nice."

For the rest of the night, Milan and I cuddled on the sofa and watched movies. There wasn't any evidence of the sudden illness that had overcome her earlier. Milan was as good as new. Later that night, she showed me how much better she felt when I inched my way deep inside her.

Chapter 31

Xavier

A couple of weeks came and went after I dropped by Dre's crib. Now my curiosity about the enigmatic Milan had definitely been piqued. It wasn't that I was jealous of their relationship, but it had been a while since Dre' had been in a serious relationship, and I was curious as to what made this chick different. My man was acting all sappy, and it wasn't a good look.

Dre' had described her as the perfect woman: beautiful, sexy, intelligent, and domestic. In my opinion she sounded too good to be true. I had learned from experience that what glittered like gold was not always gold. There was no doubt that Dre' was falling hard for her. So regardless, she was one hell of a woman to be able to do that, because we both had had our fill of beautiful women. From my experience, they were a dime a dozen.

It was now becoming my mission to meet her. I joked with Dre' that she was a figment of his imagination. He shot back that the invisible visitor in my home was a product of my imagination. Last Friday plans had been made for Dre', Milan, and me to meet for drinks. Dre' showed up. I showed up. Milan was a no-show. She called at the last minute, stating she had to go out of town on business. Didn't she know that before that day? Who told their employee at the last minute that they were needed in such and such a city? Once again, Dre' and I ended up kicking it. I noticed he wasn't looking like himself. He looked tired, with dark, puffy circles under his eyes, and he appeared thinner.

"Man, looks like you have lost some weight."

"A little."

"What's the deal? Are you working out?"

"No, I'll leave that to you."

"Man, you don't know what you're missing. We are not getting any younger. We need to stay in shape."

"I'll survive, but I haven't had a big appetite lately. I need to double up on the vitamins, because I definitely feel sluggish, like I have the flu."

"Milan is wearing your ass out." I laughed. "That's all."

"You might be right about that. She definitely knows how to please me in the bedroom. I have no complaints on my end."

"She's the perfect woman," I mocked.

"Almost."

"I'm beginning to think she doesn't want to meet me," I joked.

"We'll all eventually hook up."

"Did I tell you I spoke with Bailey?"

"No, I don't think so. What's up with her? How is she doing?"

"We didn't talk long, but she claimed her so-called accident wasn't an accident, after all."

"How so?" Dre' asked.

"Well, I always assumed she slipped and fell down the stairs at her apartment complex."

"Yeah, that's what you told me too."

"According to her, she was pushed."

"Why would someone do that?"

"Exactly. That was my question as well. I asked her if it was an attempted robbery, and she said no. The police didn't find anything missing from the fanny pack around her waist."

"Damn. There are some crazy people out there."

"Get this. She said she thought it was a female that shoved her and caused the fall."

"You're kidding. Whose husband is she fucking?"

"Man, you are not too far from the truth. Bailey said the female told her to leave *him* alone."

"Who is *him?* Does *him* have a name?" Dre' quizzed.

"According to Bailey, that's all that was said. I guess it was assumed she knew who he was."

"Well, I hope ole girl gets better soon."

"Me too, man. She has lost a lot of work, and she sounded depressed, not like the fun, loving Bailey I know."

"That's a bad break."

"Literally. Tell me about it."

"What's the deal with Miss Kendall?"

"Your guess is as good as mine. After that text I told you about, I tried texting her back and she never responded."

"Do you think she changed her mind after having second thoughts?" Dre' asked.

"Honestly, I don't know what's going on with her. I was surprised she sent the text to begin with. You know I used to tell you how uptight she was, and this was totally out of character."

"Women. You can't live with them, and you can't live without them. Who knows, maybe hubby isn't throwing down in the bedroom the way you were, and she misses that."

I nodded in agreement.

"What are you going to do?"

"Absolutely nothing. Kendall made her choice. She's married now—happily, according to her—and she wasn't even willing to try to work things out with me after she found out about Pilar."

"You weren't saying that a few weeks ago. Did she shatter that big ego?" Dre' laughed.

"No. I've had time to think. I admit I still love her, probably always will, but it's time to move on. If I can't have her totally, then I don't want her at all."

"Hmmm, that's probably what she was thinking about Pilar."

I glared at Dre', and he laughed.

"Man, you are supposed to be on my side."

"The truth hurts."

"You know what? We talk about Pilar all the time."

"We do, don't we?"

"She changed my life," I half muttered to myself.

"That she did. . . ."

"For the worse," I said.

"Claim it back," Dre' stated.

Chapter 32

Pilar

"Damn. Damn. Damn," I swore as I made my way home two weeks ago, hitting my fist on the steering wheel.

That was a close call, I thought. I hadn't seen that coming. I definitely had to be more careful until my plan was fully executed.

Xavier showing up at Dre's house out of the blue was unexpected, but I handled it well. And Dre', I had him wrapped around my pinkie finger. I had learned long ago how to read people and to become what they wanted me to be. Too bad I had to involve him in this drama to teach Xavier, with his hardheaded ass, a lesson. Oh well, such was life. Sometimes people were simply in the wrong place at the wrong time or met the wrong person. When I had arrived back at my apartment after leaving Dre's, I walked straight to the kitchen. I quickly and efficiently took out an item carefully concealed in my large black tote. The antifreeze was placed back in my cupboard, concealed behind some canned goods. It would be safe there until I needed to use a bit more. I used it only in very, very small doses and not every day. In fact, the night Xavier showed up was only the second time I had mixed a bit in Dre's drink. Antifreeze was odorless and had a sweet taste, so it blended well with iced tea, lemonade, Gatorade, and other drinks. I had done my research. It would be safe in the cupboard. No one ever visited.

Dre' had never been to my apartment, not even once. He wasn't even exactly sure where I lived. He had bought the idea hook, line, and sinker that my place was tiny and I still hadn't unpacked everything and gotten my personal belongings like I wanted. So, we always hung out at his place. Men are stupid. You could pretty much tell them anything, and they would accept it. Especially if it was told to them after they got some.

Now my biggest concern was trying to figure out how I was going to get out of dinner with Dre' and Xavier. I had already missed having drinks with them. Even with plastic surgery, Xavier would recognize me in a second. That I was sure. During the media frenzy I'd been subjected to, Dre' never met me or saw me up close.

The day of the scheduled dinner came, and I still hadn't figured out how I was going to get out of it without it being obvious. It finally dawned on me. Later that evening I waited until I knew for a fact that they were both at the restaurant. I had watched them, from a distance, arrive earlier. Xavier, as usual, took my breath away. If only he could have loved me. Dre' arrived shortly afterward. I smiled sadly. Lately, he hadn't been feeling well. He had lost a little weight because he couldn't keep much in his stomach. *Poor baby.*

I gave them ten minutes to get settled and then called Dre's cell phone. "Hey, babe," I said in my sweetest voice, which made him melt.

"Hey, where are you? Xavier and I are waiting at the restaurant."

I paused. "I'm afraid I'm going to be a little late, babe."

"Why?" I could hear the impatience in his voice. "What's going on?"

"I had a flat tire a few minutes ago. I think there may be a nail in it."

"Damn. Do you need me to change it for you?"

"No, don't be foolish. AAA will be here soon. I've already called."

"Are you sure?" Dre' asked.

"I'm positive, babe. You and Xavier go ahead and start dinner without me. I'll join you for dessert and coffee."

"This is unbelievable. I'm never going to get the two of you in the same room at the same time."

"Tell Xavier I'm sorry, but this was uncontrollable. I'm sure he'll understand."

We hung up.

I checked in a few more times, but I never made it to that damn restaurant. Dre' was upset, but what was he going to do about it? Nothing. Absolutely nothing. I couldn't come face-to-face with Xavier yet. Soon, though.

Leeda had been on my mind lately. Since I had arrived back in Houston after leaving L.A., I had a new cell phone number. Therefore, Leeda had no way of contacting me. As far as I knew, she didn't know I was back in Houston. She didn't know where I was, and I was sure that was driving her nuts. I hated to upset her, because she was the closest person to a friend, or real family, that I had. I had broken most of my ties to my mother's family years ago. My time in Houston would be finished shortly, and I couldn't wait to talk to Leeda. I knew she loved me, imperfections and all, and I had to admit I loved her, too. In many ways, she was like the mother I had always wished for.

When she was my therapist, I got to the point where I enjoyed going into her office and talking about life: my past, my present, and my future. Leeda would quietly and patiently listen. And most of all, she wouldn't judge. She understood that I didn't have a wonderful childhood or a loving mother who catered to my every need. She knew my mother didn't meet any of my needs and was, in fact, what nightmares stemmed from.

Chapter 33

Dre'

Life had a funny way of crapping on your joy. Just when things in my life were going well—I was at the peak of my career, I had met a wonderful woman, and for once, I was truly happy—life took a dump.

Milan was all I had ever wanted in a woman. We got along well, and as I got to know her, at least the pieces of her life she shared with me, I realized I was falling in love with her. I didn't ask for it, plan for it, but it was happening. It was happening rather quickly, too. That part shocked me.

Milan and I had developed a comfortable routine of sorts. Most evenings found her at my place. She would even spend the night a couple of times a week. There was nothing I enjoyed more than falling asleep with her wrapped snugly in my arms. I loved watching her sleep. Milan had extra clothes in my closet, underwear in my dresser drawer, and a toothbrush in my bathroom—all the essentials. She pretty much came and went as she saw fit, because she now had her own key to my home. I understood her need for space and privacy; I didn't trip on that.

Some evenings I would come in from work to find her in her own little world, staring blankly into space. I began to expect those mood swings. I would hold, caress, and talk to her, and soon it, whatever it was, would pass. I think it was during those times that a shift occurred and we became closer. She started opening up, telling me bits and pieces of her childhood. She told me how she and her mother didn't get along—that was putting it mildly—and how she was molested and raped as a child. That explained a lot of the sadness I saw in her eyes. Not only did her confessions break my heart, but they made me so mad that I wanted to hurt someone.

I wanted to protect her and shield her from any more pain. I could relate at some level because my mother wouldn't have won the Mother of the Year Award, either. However, I now had a better understanding of alcoholism, and I had forgiven her years ago. Milan, on the other hand, doted on me to a shameful degree. I had to admit I loved it. She was forever cooking delicious meals and buying me presents. If it was true that the key to a man's heart was through his stomach, then she had mine hook, line, and sinker.

Milan and I had been seeing each other for a few months now. Xavier wasn't around a lot, because he was doing the TV and college circuit. He had been on several of the national talk shows as an expert on stalkers and stalking. We joked that all it took to be considered an expert was to write a book on a certain topic, in his case, after surviving it. It still amazed me how much he was paid to speak at colleges and universities.

Like I said, life had a way of snatching back any happiness it gave. For the first time ever, I had health issues. For the life of me, I couldn't figure out why I was always so damn tired. I never had any energy or an appetite. Whenever I forced myself to eat, I still couldn't keep much down. Lately, all I did was sleep, sleep, sleep. Most evenings after work, after spending time with Milan, I would crash. And on the days when she was out of town on business, I'd walk in the house and make a beeline straight to my bed. I had doubled up on my vitamins but still didn't feel any better. I felt like I had a long-term case of the flu, complete with body aches and chills. I had taken all sorts of over-the-counter remedies, but I still hadn't made an appointment to see a doctor.

Since I was a child, about six or seven years old, I had always had this fear of going to the doctor. I would literally have anxiety attacks. I think I saw going to the doctor as a bad thing. I remembered when my grandmother went when she was sick and never returned home. She died there, well, actually at the hospital, but I never looked at doctors quite the same way.

Milan told me not to worry. She said she would be my personal nurse, and I believed her. Believed every word she said, like she was my personal angel.

Chapter 34

Xavier

"Bailey, think hard. Can you remember anything else that you may have forgotten to mention earlier?" I asked.

"No. It's like I told you before. I know for sure it was a female, and she was dressed from head to toe in black. She had on some type of mask, which exposed her eyes, nose, and mouth. And those eyes . . . I will never forget those eyes. They were filled with such rage and hatred. She came out of nowhere and viciously shoved me down the stairs."

"What did she say again?" I asked curiously.

"I can't remember the exact words."

"Think. This is important. What do you think she said?"

"She said that I had better leave him alone. This was just a warning."

I was quiet for a moment. Thinking.

"Xavier?"

"Yeah?"

"What is this about? Why the fifty questions?" Bailey asked.

"I'm not sure yet, but I'm trying my best to figure it out."

"You are scaring me. Do you think you know who did this?"

"Don't be afraid, but I have my suspicions."

"Who, and why?"

I hesitated. "Pilar. Because she is still stalking me."

"Are you serious? Do you realize how irrational you sound?"

"Why is it so far-fetched? Dre' said the same thing."

"Pilar would be crazy to still be around. Everyone knows the story, thanks to your movie."

"You said the key word. She would be crazy, which she is."

"Why would she attack me? I haven't done anything to her. She doesn't even know me."

"She probably thought we were a couple, and then you became a threat to her."

It was Bailey's turn to remain quiet.

"Bailey?"

"I'm here. Do you think she has been watching us?"

"I don't know what I think. Possibly."

"Creepy."

"Tell me about it. How have you been?" I asked.

She laughed halfheartedly. "I've seen better days."

"I'm sorry this happened to you."

"Me too. Life sucks."

"Things will get better. Let me know if there is anything else I can do."

She laughed. "Well, I haven't been laid in months. Can you handle that problem? Well, actually, I know you can. Real well."

I laughed along with her, but I knew I would never go back there.

"My mother has moved in because I can't take care of myself. I'm literally flat on my back. I'm missing movie opportunities left and right. It can't get much worse, but I appreciate the fact that you wired money into my account."

"You are very welcome, Bailey."

"It meant a lot since I won't be working for quite a while. Thanks to you, I'm in pretty good shape financially. I can keep my place, pay my bills, and eat without any problems. Thank you."

"You know you're my girl."

She laughed. "Yeah, me and every other girl is *your* girl. However, regardless of what people say about you, you are a good person, Xavier."

"Thank you, I think," I said.

"Seriously, Kendall should have never let you go. No one is perfect and without faults. She was a fool."

"Well, I think she would debate you on that point."

"I was willing to share you in order to at least have a piece of you."

"I'm afraid Kendall wasn't as accommodating as you. Listen, I have to run, so take care, Bailey. I'll talk to you later."

"Oh, I'm getting too serious?" She laughed. "My Xavier. My Xavier. You will never change, but I still love you, though. Bye, sweetie. Don't take so long to call next time."

I slowly hung up, trying to figure out if the unknown female could have possibly been Pilar. I simply wasn't sure. Bailey definitely got around and didn't have a lack of dates. The attacker could have been anyone, but my intuition was telling me otherwise.

I thought back to yet another encounter with Kendall a few days earlier. Talk about déjà vu. I ran into her at the mall again. This time I was searching for an outfit to wear on a local cable program I was cohosting. This time her face didn't register surprise when she saw me; this time I saw a flash of fear.

"Kendall," I said, walking up to her. "How are you?"

"Hello, Xavier," she said halfheartedly.

"What? No hug?" I asked jokingly, holding out my arms.

"No, not today," she said without cracking a single smile.

I noticed she looked tired. "What was up with that text? And when I responded, you never texted back."

"Just a moment of weakness on my part. Please, act like it never happened, because it never will again," she said coldly.

"It's like that, huh?"

She didn't respond.

"Well, it did happen, but I will respect your wishes."

"Look, Xavier. I have to go," she suddenly cried out, walking away.

I reached out and grabbed her arm. "Listen, Kendall, I didn't mean to upset you. I'm just trying to understand what's going on."

"Nothing is going on. Absolutely nothing, and it never will. I am a happily married woman. Now, let me go. Please."

I stood there, frozen in place, shocked at her unexpected reaction. I released her.

"I suggest you be careful about who you mess around with."

"What does that mean?" I asked.

"I mean you are dangerous, and I want no part of the unsavory people you attract."

"What are you talking about?"

"I probably shouldn't tell you this, but I received a warning to stay away from you, and this time I am heeding it."

"What?"

"Have a great life, Xavier. I sincerely wish you the best." And with that, she simply turned and walked away. Kendall left me standing there, more confused

than ever. I knew that would be the last time we would ever speak.

Some things were not adding up. One plus one did not equal three. I had always prided myself on paying attention to my gut instincts. It had given me an advantage and had kept my ass out of hot water numerous times in the past.

And now . . . That little inner voice we all had was telling me all was not as it seemed.

Chapter 35

Pilar

"You are truly beautiful, Milan, inside and out, and I'm thankful to have you in my life."

Those were the words spoken by Dre' as I left his place in the wee morning hours, and you know what? I believed him.

Dre' was turning out to be everything that I had never expected him to be. He was a complete contradiction to what he showed on the outside. He was a romantic, and so was I. He actually listened when I talked, and he genuinely cared for me. Unfortunately, Dre' had to become a casualty of war.

I had not given him an antifreeze-laced drink in the last few days because he would get sick with cramps and vomiting. I knew Dre' didn't deserve it, but I had to make Xavier suffer. I wanted him to lose everything—his best friend, his woman (already done), his perfect life . . . his mind. I hated Xavier so much, it hurt. He made me sick. I hated him with as much passion as I had once loved him. How dare he act like I didn't mean anything to him? How dare he act like he could screw me and toss me away, like everything was my fault?

I came to realize that there was no fixing him; he was just as damaged as I was. *Never judge a book by its cover.* Xavier looked exciting, sexy, and handsome on the outside, but on the inside, he didn't really like women. He saw us as sex objects, as opportunities to further his personal agenda; he saw us as inferior. I truly believed he couldn't ever love anyone but himself, and I knew with everything in me that he deserved to be punished. So, I decided I was going to be jury, judge, and executioner.

If only I could have a moment of peace. I found myself staying more and more at my own apartment, because I didn't want Dre' to witness my spells, as I called them. Peace had been coming less and less frequently these last few days. The voices were louder, and it was becoming difficult to control them. I didn't have much strength left. Some days I wanted to call Leeda, before I became lost in my own mind. I knew I needed to be back on my meds, but I hated them because they made me feel like the walking dead, and that was no way to live. However, without them, the voices would start to torment me.

Bitch, what do you need Leeda for? I'm the only one you have ever needed.

I'd shake my head in a frantic attempt to dispel the thoughts.

All Leeda has ever done for you is to keep you doped up like some zombie. All that talk, talk, talk she does about what a horrible mother I was. I did what I had to do for us to survive.

"Shut up! Shut up!" I screamed, pounding my forehead with my fist, leaving harsh, ugly bruises.

You know what you need to do. Get rid of Dre'. He is just like all the others. Don't let him fool you. He will say anything to stick his dirty dick inside you. How could he possibly love your ugly, skinny ass? Look at you.

"Leave me alone. I hate you. Why can't you stay in hell?"

She laughed that throaty, evil laugh that I had always despised. *You had better hush with that crying and do what you need to do. You know I can't stand those goddamn tears. Shut it up, and get it done.*

Chapter 36

Dre'

"I love you, Milan." Yes, I said it, and I really meant it. Milan had come into my life, and for once I was happy. I didn't feel the need to chase after other women. She was all I needed and then some. She took care of me and allowed me to be a man. There was rarely any drama, yet she spoke her mind. Even with my sudden health issues, she stuck by my side, caring for me during my time of need.

She didn't respond when I said those words to her. In fact, she remained silent and her face lit up for a few moments and then a sadness fell upon her.

"Are you okay, baby?"

"I couldn't be better. I just realized this is what it sounds like when it's sincere. No man, not one, has ever told me they loved me and really meant it."

"That's almost impossible to believe."

"Sadly, it's true."

"Well, I love you, and it's real, because I feel it deep within my heart every time I see you or hear your voice," I said, wrapping my arms securely around her. She fit perfectly.

With that, she started crying. Deep, heavy sobs.

"Baby? What did I say?"

Between cries she said, "How can you love me?"

"How could I not?"

"I'm damaged. If only you knew of my childhood and some of the terrible things that were done to me. I've shared only surface things with you, and I'm no angel. I've done some horrible things in my lifetime."

"Baby, I don't hold your past against you. We are all products of our environment in one way or another, and we are all imperfect beings. I've done many misdeeds in my lifetime as well. I don't cast stones."

She cried, looking deep into my eyes, struggling to believe my words.

"I've told you about my childhood, hanging out in the streets and living with a single mother who drank too much. My life hasn't been a cakewalk, either. You have to learn to trust people and lean on them sometimes when you're weak. I will never hurt you, Milan. I promise you that."

With those words, even more sobs came. I had sensed Milan had been abused far worse than she had revealed to me. I'd see it in her eyes at the most inopportune moments. Her smiles and laughter never met her eyes. The eyes knew. They were the mirrors to the soul.

I was truthful in what I said. I would never hurt her. I only wanted her to be happy for once. I held her for most of that night. She cried and I caressed her. I wanted my strength to flow through her, envelop her, so that she never had to be afraid again. I wanted her cries in her sleep and her nightmares to go away forever. For once, I wanted her to feel safe, sound, and protected. A side of me knew she hadn't felt that way in quite a long time, if ever.

Milan drifted asleep in my arms, and I stayed awake and watched her sleep most of the night. She cried out a few times, but I simply pulled her closer, warding off her night frights and phantoms.

Chapter 37

Xavier

"City and state?"

"Baltimore, Maryland. Do you have a listing for Dr. Leeda Smith?" I asked the operator as I held my breath in anticipation.

"Yes, sir. Please hold for that number. The number is . . ."

I quickly copied the number down and proceeded to call Dr. Smith's office. This was something I should have done long ago.

Recently, there had been more strange occurrences in my home. Crazy voices at night, items disappearing and then reappearing a couple of days later. I even received a dozen roses with a note that read: *Enjoy your success now because it's about to come to an end. The truth will set you free.*

When I located the flower shop that had made the delivery, one of the clerks vaguely remembered an attractive woman placing the order, and she paid in cash. Therefore, there wasn't a contact name or address. She couldn't remember much more.

Dr. Smith was the psychiatrist who had treated Pilar over the years. From my understanding, they had developed a doctor-patient, parent-daughter relationship. I truly felt Pilar was somehow behind the strange incidents that had been happening in my life lately.

Bailey's so-called accident and then Kendall's strange behavior . . . Something was up, and it had *Pilar* written all over it.

The line rang a couple of times, and I nervously held my breath, urging someone to pick up.

"Dr. Leeda Smith's office. How may I help you?" a cheery receptionist stated.

"This is Xavier Preston speaking. It is very urgent that I speak with Dr. Smith."

"Are you a patient, sir?"

"No, I'm not."

"Well, Mr. . ."

"Preston."

"Well, Mr. Preston, Dr. Smith is currently with a patient, and I'm afraid her schedule is full for the remainder of the day, with appointments. May I take a message and have her call you back?"

"This is of an urgent nature, and it's imperative that I speak to her as soon as possible. Perhaps she can call me in between patients."

"May I ask what this pertains to?"

I hesitated for a few seconds.

"Pilar."

"Is there a last name?" she questioned.

"She'll know exactly who I'm talking about."

"Your name again?"

"Xavier Preston, and I can be reached at five-five-five-zero-one-zero-zero. Please have her call me ASAP."

The next thirty minutes were probably the longest of my life. I paced back and forth, making a trail from the kitchen to the living room. I couldn't sit; I was too antsy. When the landline rang, my heart leapt to my throat and I literally froze for a moment.

With two quick steps, I ran to pick up the receiver.

"May I speak with Xavier Preston?" a professional, pleasant-sounding female voice asked.

"This is he."

"Hello, Mr. Preston. This is Dr. Smith returning your call."

"Thank goodness," I cried. I didn't waste any time with pleasantries; I dove headfirst into my problem. "I need to ask you something."

"You sound a little frantic. Is everything okay, Mr. Preston? You mentioned in your message that you had questions pertaining to Pilar."

"No, everything isn't okay. Have you seen her? Are you in contact with Pilar?"

"No, actually, I haven't heard from her in months."

"Do you know where she is?"

"No, I don't."

"Are you sure, Dr. Smith? This is very important. I think Pilar is here in Houston."

"That can't be correct. The last time I talked to her, she was in L.A."

"She was in L.A.? Why?"

"I'm sorry, Mr. Preston, but I'm sure you understand that I can't discuss any information concerning Pilar with you. I made a mistake by telling you she was in L.A."

"Damn! Recently, I was in L.A., completing my movie project."

"I know. I've followed your success the last couple of years. A person can't help but see your name and the movie title plastered everywhere. What's the nature of your questions, may I ask?"

"I think Pilar may be here in Houston, stalking me again."

"What makes you say that? Has something happened? Has she contacted you?"

"No. Not yet, anyway, but little things have occurred that don't add up."

"Like what, may I ask?"

"Female friends of mine have been threatened and assaulted. Personal items have disappeared and then reappeared in different locations in my home, and I hear strange sounds inside my home. My assistant, Khai, is afraid to stay in my house by herself. The other day I received an anonymous flower delivery with a cryptic message," I gushed without a pause.

"Hmmm."

"I know it doesn't sound like much, but I have my suspicions, and they all lead directly to Pilar. If she is following me, could she be off her meds and dangerous? Could she be the one who assaulted my friends?"

"I can't answer that, but it doesn't stop you from drawing your own conclusions about her harming your friends and still being a danger to you," Dr. Smith stated in her calm, reassuring tone.

"Wow! If this ain't some shit!" I exclaimed.

"Just stay levelheaded, Mr. Preston. I'm sure you'll get to the bottom of this."

"No disrespect, Dr. Smith, but that's easy for you to say. You should have had her crazy ass locked up years ago. She's a danger to society and those around her."

"I understand your concern, but you aren't sure if she is behind your recent occurrences, and no bodily harm has come to you."

"Are you fucking kidding? Not yet. Have you forgotten what she did to me in the hotel with that mini whip? And what about my friends? They haven't done anything to her."

"No, I haven't forgotten, Mr. Preston. I apologize if I come across as unconcerned, because that is truly not my desire, but I have a physician-patient privilege to uphold. I'm sure you understand."

"Well, if you just happen to speak with that bitch, make her *understand* that I will never be the man she thinks I am. I don't want her, and never in a million years will that change."

"You have made yourself perfectly clear. Take care, Mr. Preston."

With that I slowly hung up the phone. "Damn. She could be in Houston."

Chapter 38

Pilar

Creative Writing 101 teaches that every book has a dramatic climax. For Xavier, Dre', and I, it happened on a balmy Friday evening. We had reached our peak, and there was nowhere to go but straight down now. Something or someone had to give. I remember being very calm, because every fiber of my being told me that that day would be the day I came face-to-face with Xavier again. I was ready. More than ready. The question was, was he?

Thursday I had stayed over at Dre's house all day and night. After lunchtime, he suddenly became violently ill and took to his bed. He looked horrible, like he was on his deathbed. I decided to stay by his side, even though at that point he probably didn't even realize I was there to begin with.

I had to change his sheets twice because Dre' was a complete mess. He had it coming out of both ends. Shitting and vomiting. I almost felt sorry for him. Almost. The fact that Xavier would be overcome with grief made me overlook Dre's obvious pain and suffering. At lunchtime Friday, he refused to eat the soup I attempted to feed him or drink his Gatorade. He was very weak, and I knew he couldn't last much longer.

To my credit, I didn't leave his side. I sat quietly by in the chair I had pulled up to his bedside and read a book. I took great delight in reading passages of *Diary of a Stalker* by Xavier Preston. All it did was nurture my furor. Yeah, he would pay soon, and he would finally learn the lesson.

Dre's cell phone, which rested on the nightstand, rang several times throughout the day, but Dre' was in no condition to answer it. As he rested, I checked his voice mail.

"Hey, man, I called your job, and they told me you haven't been in for a few days. You never get sick. You are healthy as a horse. What's up? Hit me up."

Then later: "Dre', call me. I need to speak with you about something, or should I say, someone."

Then finally: "Man, you are scaring me. Call me. Okay? If I don't hear from you soon, I'm going to come by and check on you."

I deleted his messages and went back to reading, humming a tune as I stroked Dre's cheek. He was burning up with fever. It was the calm before the storm. My body was alive with anticipation. I felt like I was being pricked with tiny needles.

"I'm so sorry, Dre'. I hated to do this to you, babe, but Xavier left me no choice. He made me do this. That's your friend," I whispered into the warm air comprised of moans and groans.

Dre' didn't respond; he simply tossed and turned, trying to get relief from his pain.

"Don't worry, babe. It will be over soon, I promise." I waited patiently to come face-to-face with Xavier.

Around six thirty that evening, the doorbell rang. I didn't move. I knew exactly who was at the door, but I didn't hear anything for a few minutes. I figured he was checking out Dre's car, which was still parked in the garage. I didn't try to hide anything. I wanted him to bear witness to what he had made me do. About fifteen minutes later, after the landline and cell phones had rung continuously, I heard the front door being opened. That was no surprise, either. Dre' had told me Xavier had a key and the code to his alarm system.

I slowly got up from my chair and made myself invisible in the shadows over near the closet. It was time for the final act. Only faint light from the sole bedroom window peeked through, casting an eerie glow upon the fragile figure of Dre', slumped in bed, tangled among the sweat-drenched sheets. I had already pulled the lone chair away and placed the book upon Dre's heaving chest. The stage was set. It was showtime.

I heard him slowly making his way up the stairs. He took slow, confident steps. He didn't call out Dre's name. I think he somehow sensed me; we were so in tune with one another now. I could picture the worried expression on his handsome face as he made his way to check on his best friend in the world. I was going to show him who he was messing with, and he wouldn't underestimate me again.

I smelled him before I saw him. His masculine cologne inched its way into the room before he did. My heart leapt in my chest, and a lump formed in the back of my throat. This was the moment I had waited for. The moment I had played over and over in my mind. The moment I had planned for months.

I savored the expression on his face, one I would always cherish, as he saw Dre's anguish and crumpled form in bed. He ran to his bedside, but before he could reach him, I stepped forward, out of the shadows, with the twelve-inch blade extended in my right hand. A gun wouldn't do. This was personal. Xavier had made it personal.

"Hello, Xavier," I said and smiled sweetly.

The surprise on his face was absolutely priceless.

"We meet again. We really have to stop meeting under such tragic circumstances," I stated, stepping closer and showing him the shiny blade. My demeanor convinced him I wasn't playing.

Even with my surgery, he knew who I was. Xavier hadn't forgotten me, and after today he never would. I witnessed various expressions cross his face in a matter of mere seconds. I couldn't help but smile. Time stood still. I was in the same room as Xavier Preston, and I was in control. I felt wonderful and powerful.

"It's me, babe, Pilar, also known as Milan to your buddy over there," I added, pointing to Dre'. "Surprise, surprise."

Xavier didn't utter a single word. I think for once I had rendered him speechless. His eyes darted back and forth, from me holding the knife to Dre' moaning and writhing on the bed.

"Did you miss me yet?" I asked and started to laugh with total glee. It brought me such joy to be in his presence. Xavier was such a sexy man, and he never ceased to take my breath away. Even now, if he simply apologized, I would probably forgive and forget.

"Pilar, this isn't funny," he said in a very calm voice. With his hands at his sides, he was trying hard to maintain his composure. I knew this man like the back of my own hands, and he was trying hard to stay cool and collected.

"Oh, this is funny. You should see your face," I said, taking a step closer to Dre'. I laughed wholeheartedly, clutching my stomach.

"I knew you were back. What do you want from me?" Xavier asked, holding up his hands.

"What do you want from me?" I mocked. "I want your soul, Xavier." I laughed again.

"I'm serious, Pilar. I'll do—"

"Shut the fuck up, Xavier. It's too late for all your bullshit. Just shut up. I don't want to hear your pathetic lies. Don't you understand, it's too late?"

"It's not too late. It's never too late. Let me call an ambulance for Dre', and then you and I can talk. Let's get Dr. Smith on the line," he said, looking at Dre' again, concern etching his face and causing frown lines to crease his forehead.

"Do you think you are dealing with a fool? Well, babe, news flash, you are not! Pretty soon Dre' won't need an ambulance or anyone else, including you. All he'll need is a box buried six feet under. And leave Leeda out of this."

I saw him slowly begin to lose control. His hands were now balled into tight fists at his sides. "What did you do to him, bitch?"

"Oh, Xavier. Sticks and stones may break my bones, but your words will never hurt me. I love you too much."

"Dear God, what did I do to deserve this?" he screamed. "What did you do to him? He adored your crazy ass, and you do this?"

"Tsk, tsk, tsk," I said. "Stop being so damn emotional. Isn't that what you used to tell me? It doesn't become you, Xavier. It detracts from that macho image you portray. And besides, we both know you can only love yourself. You self-absorbed, egomaniacal, no-good motherfucker."

"That's right. It's me you hate, Pilar. Why bring Dre' into this?"

"Because you love him, and I want to show you how it feels to lose someone you love with all your heart."

"Dre' has been nothing but kind to you. How can you do this to him? Please, let me call an ambulance. I'm begging you. If not for me, then do it for him."

"Again, do you think I'm a fool, Xavier? Not." I laughed, scraping the blade over the surface of the nightstand. "I guess I was a fool for you. Letting you have your way with me, thinking we had a future together, and you, you just threw it all away . . . like it meant nothing to you . . . like I was discarded waste. Why did you do that?"

"I'm very sorry, Pilar. I don't know what else to say."

"I don't want your sorries. It's too late for that now. Were you sorry when you wrote that damn screenplay and released it to the country, full of lies, lies, lies?" I screamed, slamming the blade into the thick wood of the nightstand.

"Calm down," Xavier said.

"Were you sorry then? I can't hear you, Xavier. Speak up."

Xavier didn't respond. I saw his eyes seeking out a way for him to take me down. I knew he could overpower me if he wanted to, but I was going down with a fight to the finish.

"Make my day, Xavier. You are bigger and stronger than I am, but I'm not going out without putting a serious hurting to your ass or Dre's. Make my fucking day. I dare you."

I knew my words would make him back down. Out of the corner of my eye, I saw Dre' attempting to speak. I couldn't look at him, because I knew his eyes revealed hurt and pain. I was all too familiar with that.

"Do you see what you've made me do to your friend? Look at him. Look closely, Xavier, because this is all your fucking fault. Antifreeze poisoning is a real bitch. I read that it is an agonizing, slow death."

"I'm here to make it all better," he said softly.

"I wish that was true," I whispered. "I really do."

"Trust me."

"Trust you? Are you serious? I wouldn't trust you farther than I could throw you. Besides, you can't make it better. Don't you understand that you can't? You are going to lose Dre', just like you lost the woman you loved, along with your new playthang."

"If I could get my hands on you, I'd—"

"You'd what, babe? Kill me? I enjoyed every minute of mixing small doses of antifreeze in his drinks, because I knew this day would eventually come, when you and I came face-to-face again. I would give Dre' small breaks, long enough for him to think he was getting better, and then I would start the process all over again with my special cocktail."

"You are crazy."

"You made me this way," I shouted back.

"No, you had issues long before you ever met me, bitch. Don't give me that much credit. You deserve that all by yourself." He paused for a moment. "What did you do to your face?"

"I thought you would like this one better."

"You are totally insane," he said, nearly whispering it to himself.

"Why couldn't you simply love me?" I asked, walking closer to him, closing the gap. "I would have done anything for you, you know that, and then you betrayed me with that movie. I really thought after I dropped the assault charges and after you got off, you would grow up and realize what a great woman I am."

"Are you kidding? You disgust me. You make me sick."

I laughed. "Sticks and stones, Xavier."

Suddenly Xavier started to move his hands toward his pockets.

"What are you doing?"

"I'm going to reach in my pocket and pull out my cell phone."

"Oh no, you are not. You do that, and that will be the last thing you reach for. Understand clearly that I am running this show."

He slowly lowered his hands so that I could see them.

"That's a good boy. Did your playthang tell you what I did to her? You should have seen how she tumbled down those stairs like a rag doll. Poor baby. I don't think I've ever seen a body twisted up the way hers was. I bet it hurt like hell."

He remained silent and clenched his jaw muscles.

"She wasn't anything to you, though. I realize that now. Bailey was someone you enjoyed fucking with no commitment. Sounds familiar." I laughed. "I guess much like me, huh? You should take lessons from Dre' about commitment. You can't play for free. Pussy always comes with a price."

I reached over and stroked Dre's warm cheek and kissed him on his dry, crusty lips.

"Leave him alone!"

"You don't tell me what to do, and I can touch my man. You remember how I touched you, don't you?" I said softly.

Xavier didn't answer.

"You loved for me to suck your beautiful black dick."

"You are sick."

"Dre' could fuck, but not as well as you, babe. There is something magical about what hangs between your legs, or maybe I just love dark chocolate more. It just melts in your mouth. What do you think?"

"Please, Pilar."

"Please, Pilar. Please, Pilar," I mocked. "Is that all you can say? You make me sick. I hate your ass so much, Xavier. Oooh, you just don't know."

"Let him go," he said quietly.

"Did the love of your miserable life tell you what happened to her?"

"Huh?"

"Oh, I have your full attention now. Mention that fucking bitch Kendall, and I finally get your full attention, huh? Well, poor baby got to experience thug love. From what I understand, she was pretty wet for my boy. He had her wide open, literally. Maybe she likes those roughnecks behind closed doors, though, because she's too much of a stuck-up snob to be seen in public with one. You think?"

"You fucking bitch."

"I've been called worse. Your cute little assistant, she's a scared little thing. I enjoyed messing with her. Oh, by the way, I love the improvements you've made to your home, but your security system sucks," I said, blindly stroking Dre's cheek.

"Why, I'll—"

"Do absolutely nothing but stand there like the little bitch you are," I said, putting the blade to Dre's chin. "Don't make me go there, because you know I will."

He calmed down.

"That's what I thought. You ain't going to do nothing. Not a damn thing, but stand there like the punk you are. You lame-ass, womanizing piece of shit."

"Pilar, this isn't going to change a damn thing. You and I will never be together. I don't love you. I never have and never will. I don't want you. In fact, I don't even like you. It's taking all I have not to puke in your face. You're pathetic and disgusting. Now what?"

With those words, something inside of me burst loose like a raging dam. I snapped. It was like everything my mother had said to me over the years came rushing forth. I was sick and tired of being insulted, spoken down to, and abused.

I lunged for Xavier, with the blade aimed straight for his heart. I wanted to cut it out, stomp on it, and shred it to pieces, since he never used it, anyway. However, I managed only to cut his face. Droplets of blood spilled forth. Initially, I had an element of surprise when I lunged for him, but that was very short-lived. We wrestled around the room, knocking over anything that crossed our path. I developed superhuman strength, running on adrenaline, and I somehow managed to hold on to the knife. I knew if Xavier took it away from me, it was over. Everything.

Xavier dipped, dived, and rolled as I cursed, swinging the blade back and forth in a frenzied motion as I attempted to back him into a corner. I wanted to cut his balls off and stuff them in his lying mouth. Make him gag on them.

"I'll show you," I screamed. "I hate you. I hate you. I hate you so much."

I was now alternating between screaming and crying. It took a few minutes to realize tears were streaming down my face. I thought I was all cried out over him.

"I guess I showed your ex, huh?" I laughed in his face. "Stuck-up, bourgeois bitch got exactly what she deserved. My only regret was that I wasn't there to bear witness."

With those words, Xavier lunged at me, and we ended up on the bed, near where Dre' lay. We were fighting as if our lives depended upon it, and I guess they did. I was screaming, kicking, scratching, fighting for my life like an alley cat backed in a corner.

"You are not going to keep coming into my life and hurting the ones I love. This is going to stop today," Xavier screamed as he punched me in the face. "Do you hear me? This shit ends now."

To avoid his hits, I turned my head several times and was staring directly at Dre'. His eyes spoke of everything he couldn't say verbally. I saw pain, regret, betrayal, and just a glimpse of love. That was the last thing I remembered before my world went black. I glimpsed love. Xavier sent a right clip to my jawline, and it was lights out. Everything went black.

Chapter 39

Dre'

Life is a bitch! But I was a survivor. It had been six months since that tragic day, a day I would never forget as long as I lived.

Speaking of living, most of my doctors called me the miracle man. It was a true miracle I survived to tell my story. I guess as they say, it just wasn't my time. I was still here for a reason, a purpose yet to be revealed to me. However, I guess that was all in God's time.

I would never be the same. There would be no going back. Besides the emotional trauma, I would have long-term medical problems that would remain with me until the day I died. I just took one day at a time. That was all I could manage right now.

Xavier and I were still thicker than thieves. Hell, he basically saved my life. But . . . There was always the "elephant" in the room with us now, mainly Pilar, or Milan, as I would always remember her. We didn't discuss her, or at least we tried not to. Yet she was always with us. She was this unspeakable, invisible, intangible being that hovered around and made its presence known.

Of course, the story broke, and there was a huge media frenzy, possibly as big as before. However, this time I was brought into the mix. All our lives were dissected for the nation to see and inspect. People took sides. It was ugly. As with any news, we soon became old news.

Our story finally died down, and life gradually returned to normal. Well, as normal as it would ever be. My life was forever changed.

As much as our bond had strengthened, the elephant in the room somehow separated Xavier and me. I didn't know if the rift would ever be mended. I only hoped our friendship and history together would help us survive the aftermath of the storm.

You see, I didn't blame Milan/Pilar. My feelings were the same. I loved her. I realized most people found that very hard to believe and digest after all she had done to me, but I did. I loved Milan, and I understood she was very sick. I understood how she became what she was. I empathized with her needs and what frightened and pushed her buttons.

Many people didn't agree, some called me crazy, and others would never understand. That was fine. I tried not to sweat the small stuff now. I had been to the valley of the shadow of death, and I had survived. The public saw the media clips and believed what they saw and read. They thought Pilar was simply a monster. Her disease was the monster.

In the beginning, I saw a side of her that was capable of love. I saw her vulnerable, and she shared some of her secrets with me. Even though she attempted to hurt Xavier through me, I still felt that somewhere deep, deep inside, she cared for me. I knew what I felt.

I forgave her. I supported her. And I continued to love her. I only hoped Xavier would, in time, come to understand.

Chapter 40

Xavier

It had been six long months since that tragic day. For me, it had been déjà vu all over again, and the media had had another field day, with our photos and backstory splashed all over the place. We couldn't get away from them. They had literally camped out in front of my home in order to get a photo or quote. I had never understood America's fascination with tragedy and drama. But then again, that was what I wrote about. However, I wrote mostly fiction, but living through the real deal wasn't quite as entertaining.

I wrote, wrote, and wrote to cleanse my soul. It felt good to purge my feelings. Writing had literally become my salvation. Plus, I was seeing a therapist now. There were days I thought I was going to lose my mind; I couldn't sleep, I couldn't eat, and I couldn't function. All I wanted to do was hurt someone, mainly Pilar. It scared me that I hated another human being so much, and I hated myself because I had allowed her to reenter my life and almost destroy people I cared about. I still blamed myself for bringing her into their lives. They didn't deserve any of this.

I would never forget, as long as I lived, the sight of her hovering over Dre' like a wild predator ready to pounce and devour its prey. When I did sleep for a few hours, that was one of the haunting images I always saw and relived. As much as I hated to admit it, Pilar and I were connected for life. Every time I looked in the mirror at the small scar on my cheek, I was reminded of her. Of what she did to me. Of how she changed my life.

Dre' would never be the same. He had a few lingering ailments from the poisoning. Every time I looked at him, I felt guilt. He and I had many issues to address that we didn't speak of right now. Yet I needed him just as much as he needed me. We were much like survivors of a war; we had our war stories and scars, and that bonded us in ways no one could ever understand. We had walked through the fire and survived. I wished I could say unscathed; however, life was usually not that accommodating.

I didn't and couldn't understand some of Dre's decisions regarding her, so we didn't discuss her. I just knew I loved him like a brother, and we'd get past this, too. It was just another life problem we had to get through, and it wasn't going to be a walk in the park this time. I tried to pretend Pilar was simply a figment of my imagination, but she showed up in my nightmares.

Every week, like clockwork, they arrived. I received a letter from her. Sometimes they were long; sometimes short; sometimes frantic, almost illegible. They all had a common theme: Pilar's undying love for me. I finally gave up trying to stop them from coming. She always managed to manipulate someone to smuggle them out and mail them for her.

She scared me. I could honestly admit that. I only prayed—which was something I was doing a lot of lately—she would remain locked up for the rest of her natural life. I knew with certainty that that was the only way she would get the help she needed and I'd have a normal life, free of her. Regrets? Yeah, I had many. For the first time, I was thinking about woulda, coulda, shoulda. Now it was too late. It took only one person to change your life forever. Sometimes they came with a big butt and a smile.

Chapter 41

Pilar

They couldn't keep me locked up forever. Sooner or later, I would get out. I was very patient.

I was also smart. I always had been. I knew what they liked to hear; it was not too hard to figure out. I had always known how to play the game, and fortunately for me, I knew how to manipulate people. So, I smiled sweetly and told them what they wanted to hear.

Yes, Doctor, I understand why I became obsessed with Xavier. Yes, I understand how my childhood affected my image of myself and relationships in general. Yes, I now understand that he doesn't love me and I can't be with him.

Leeda was my ally and looked out for me. We shared the same city now, and she even paid my expenses for the best treatment possible. Dre' visited at least once a month. He was sweet, much like a new puppy.

Was I sorry about the people I hurt? Not really. We were all indispensable when it came down to it. Growing up, no one ever saved me or showed me any mercy. So why should I? Xavier, I saw him on TV, and he looked good. He was wearing a beard. Probably to hide the scar. He should realize he could try to hide it, but it was still just below the surface, a permanent part of him. My mark. Masking it didn't get rid of it. I felt that he had finally learned the lesson this time around. I gave him an A+. So maybe, just maybe, there was hope for us, after all. No one said that life was easy. Even soul mates had to go through their difficult times, too. Wasn't it Oprah who said we had to turn our wounds into wisdom?

I took out a pen and a sheet of lined notebook paper, both smuggled in by staff for a small fee. I hated that the paper couldn't be nice, expensive stationery, but I had learned long ago to deal with what was thrown my way.

I wrote:

> *Dear Xavier,*
> *Someday we will be together. I promise you that, babe. No one and no circumstances can keep us apart. You know that now. Don't you? We were meant to be together; we've been together in other lifetimes. And I've loved you every single time with just as much passion.*
> *I would die for you, babe. I would literally lay down my life to be with you.*
> *With all my love,*
Pilar

I smiled sweetly as I placed the note in the plain envelope addressed to Xavier Preston and planted a sweet kiss on it.

Questions for Discussion

1. What are your thoughts on the way Xavier treated the women in his life?

2. What do you think of Bailey and Kendall?

3. Where do you think Xavier's *rules* stemmed from? Were they effective?

4. At the beginning of the novel, was Xavier acting paranoid regarding Pilar?

5. Would surviving a traumatic experience, such as stalking, affect the way a person deals with other people?

6. Was Xavier somewhat jealous of the relationship Dre' and Milan shared?

7. Was Dre' really in love with Milan? If so, why?

8. At some point, should Dre' have been suspicious of who Milan really was?

9. Did Milan love Dre' at all, in her own way?

10. What do you think of Pilar? Do you feel sorry for her?

Questions For Discussion

11. What do you think about the extremes measures Pilar took to exact revenge on Xavier?

12. Will Pilar ever be well again?

13. Do you think Xavier and Dre' will remain friends?

14. What do you think of Dre's feelings toward Milan/ Pilar at the end of the story?

15. Will Xavier ever be free of Pilar?

16. Do you think Xavier will settle down, marry, and have a family?

17. Will you go back and read *Diary of a Stalker* to find out how this stalker story began, when Pilar and Xavier first met?